One Mixed-Up Night

One Mixed-Up Night

CATHERINE NEWMAN

Random House • New York

Text copyright © 2017 by Catherine Newman
Jacket art copyright © 2017 by Ann Macarayan

Visit us on the Web! randomhousekids.com

Educators and librarians, for a variety of teaching tools, visit us at
RHTeachersLibrarians.com

Library of Congress Cataloging-in-Publication Data
Names: Newman, Catherine, author.
Title: One mixed-up night / Catherine Newman.
Description: First edition. | New York : Random House, [2017] |
Summary: "Unbeknownst to their parents, twelve-year-olds Frankie
and Walter spend the night in an IKEA store"—Provided by publisher.
Identifiers: LCCN 2016044700 |
ISBN 978-0-399-55388-2 (hardcover) |
ISBN 978-0-399-55390-5 (ebook) |
ISBN 978-0-399-55389-9 (lib. bdg.)
Subjects: | CYAC: Best friends—Fiction. | Friendship—Fiction. |
Stores, Retail—Fiction. | Family life—Fiction.
Classification: LCC PZ7.1.N4855 One 2017 | DDC [Fic]—dc23

The text of this book is set in 12.25-point Berling.
Interior design by Jaclyn Whalen

Printed in the United States of America
10 9 8 7 6 5 4 3 2 1
First Edition

Random House Children's Books supports the First Amendment and
celebrates the right to read.

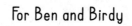
For Ben and Birdy

CONTENTS

One Mixed-Up Night

1

The Parents Make a Plan

The funny thing is this: people think that dorky geeks who read all the time are the kinds of kids who don't get into trouble. But they're wrong. We do. And I'm telling you this from experience. I'm telling you this because there was a moment when Walter and I were scrunched into a pair of hanging chairs in the Ikea showroom at four in the morning, thrilled and terrified, hiding from the security guard with her walkie-talkie, and I thought, *We wouldn't even be here if we hadn't read the books we've read.*

Which was true.

But let me back up, because the story doesn't start

there. It starts with my family and Walter's family sitting at our dinner table with the pizza plates pushed aside, trying to figure out if it was worth schlepping to Ikea for the various things we were all wanting. Walter is my oldest friend, and our parents are best friends—or whatever the grown-up equivalent is—and we always say that if Walter's cat, Puddle, met my cat, Mr. Pockets, they'd be best friends too. When we were little, we actually used to draw pictures of them getting married, the two cats in their tuxedos because they're both boys, me and Walter holding the little rings.

"Maybe you and I can just make a run down there so everyone doesn't have to go," my mom was saying to Walter's mom. "It seems silly to drag two carloads of people for some picture frames and a slipcover."

"And the shoe bench," Walter's mom said.

"And the patio table," my dad said.

"And the hangers and file boxes and that thing we wanted for the bathroom, for the towels to go somewhere," Walter's mom said.

"And the things I want, which are lots of things, lots of different things that I don't even know what they *are* because I don't even know what there *is*," Walter's little brother, Zeke, said. He's three, in case that wasn't obvious.

But wait, I'm sorry, because maybe you don't even know what Ikea is! Poor you! Let me tell you. Ikea is this ginormous chain of Swedish furniture stores. Which sounds totally unfun, I know, but somehow everything they sell is crazily nice and you want it: all this furniture that looks really clean and modern, and it's made of pretty wood that's perfectly light or perfectly dark, or it's painted some awesome color so you feel like if you had it in your house, you'd be living inside a TV show about people with really nice houses, if you know what I mean. But they sell all this other stuff too—dishes and posters and lamps and toys—and everything is cool and appealing, and you want it, even though it would be hard to say why. But it's kind of cheap enough that sometimes you can convince grown-ups to buy you something. We've only been to the actual store a couple of times, though. Mostly, Walter and I just lie around with the Ikea catalog at his house or mine, wanting things.

Now Walter said, "No offense, but it would be dumb for you to go yourselves because you don't even *like*

Ikea! And Frankie and I love it." *Frankie* is short for *Francesca*, which nobody has ever called me except, apparently, my Italian grandmother. But she died when I was a baby, and since then it's been Frankie always and only.

"That's a good point," my mom said. My mom, who actually looked into ordering Ikea stuff *online* instead of going there! (Luckily, it's weirdly hard and expensive to have it delivered.) Which makes her very different from me and Walter, because we would seriously go to Ikea every single day. Instead, we look at the catalog. Like, *all the time.*

Sometimes my mom squashes onto the old gray couch to peer at the Ikea stuff with us. "What are you two drooling over now?" And we point to this or that living room, everything all clean and kind of fancily plain, with no colored pencils or pencil sharpeners or pencil shavings scattered across the old coffee table along with the Spirograph pieces. No cloud-shaped stain on the rug where Mr. Pockets had horked up a massive hair ball full of colored-pencil shavings. No shredded couch armrests where Mr. Pockets has been sharpening his claws his entire life. No perfectly unused scratching post next to the torn-up couch.

"I have two solutions," Mom said one time. "And

they're both free! Give away all your stuff, and get rid of Mr. Pockets. Then it'll be just like we're living in a showroom!"

I knew she wasn't even half-serious. She likes Spirograph, for one thing, and for another, Mr. Pockets is the love of her life. That's what she always says when he's lying on her chest, purring into her face. "Who's the love of my life? Is it you? Is it you? Yes. It's you." And my father always clears his throat really loudly—"A-a-a-hem"—which makes her laugh.

Anyway, at the dinner table, Walter and I started making our case for a big two-family Ikea trip. Walter— and I'm not just saying this because he's my best friend (even though I *would* just say it because he's my best friend)—has one of those dimply, long-eyelashed faces that makes everybody pretty much need to let him do whatever it is he's hoping to do. Including me. I mean, I can hardly ever say no to him, but that's fine, because he hardly ever asks for anything I would want to say no to.

"It's almost my birthday," Walter was saying now (dimple, dimple), "and maybe we could just do my dinner celebration there with these guys. That's my first choice, and it would be totally cheap and easy."

"As long as it's cheap and easy," his mom, Alice, teased. "We don't really want to go all out on your birthday, Walter. A fast, inexpensive Swedish meal at the Ikea food court. That's about as far as I'm willing to stretch."

Walter laughed. His mom once hand-made a papier-mâché piñata in the shape of Harry Potter's wizard hat and filled it with foil-wrapped chocolate wands. Going all out on his birthday was kind of a family tradition.

My mom put out a plate of the pink candy-cane fudge she was trying to get perfect. She's a food writer for a magazine, and we spend our lives eating delicious things in the wrong season because they need to be figured out so far ahead of time. "Recipe testing?" Alice asked, taking a piece, and my mom nodded.

Alice took a bite.

"Grainy?" my mom asked.

"A little grainy," my dad said, biting into his piece. "You can feel the sugar crystals on your tongue. But not in a bad way. I think that's just what fudge is like."

Walter's mom shrugged and reached for another piece. "It tastes perfect to me."

"It tastes *fudgy* to me," Zeke said seriously, the fudge already spreading across his face like a pink beard. Then he added, like my dad, "Not in a bad way."

"Guys," Walter said. "Guys. Seriously. Ikea." He was trying to refocus the grown-ups, who sometimes have super-short attention spans. "Plus, then I can use Grandma's birthday money to get that cool spinning desk chair. Which I really, really want. Please?"

And the parents did their special Parental Silent Communication—raised eyebrows, eye contact around the table, shrugging—and just like that, it was decided.

"Saturday?" my dad said. "It'll be a madhouse, but that's probably the only day we're all free."

"Okay to meet after lunch?" my mom asked. "I'm going to have to finish recipe notes and drop off samples in the morning."

"Perfect," Alice said, taking Zeke's hand and holding it gently in her two hands to, I think, stop him from taking a third piece of fudge. "We can shop a little, get some dinner, finish up before they close." She asked me if I wanted to come home with them after Ikea to spend the night, which I did.

"Or Walter could spend the night here," my mom

said, "so the kids can help me recipe-test the eggnog waffles I'm supposed to be inventing."

"Either way," Walter and I said at exactly the same time, and Alice said, "We can figure it out later."

Which was definitely the grown-ups' first mistake.

2

We Make a Plan Too
(At Least Sort Of)

Ikea had been written on our calendar, by me, in big blue letters. Saturday, May 17. It was now Thursday the fifteenth, and Walter was over after school. We were lying in my family's red-and-pink-striped hammock, under the big maple tree, and we were eating popcorn—really buttery and salty, the way we both like it—looking at the Ikea catalog and playing the "picking game." You probably play it too, even if you call it something else: it's the game where you look at a catalog with someone, and you each pick the thing you most want from every page. I like playing with Walter because I can almost always guess what he's going to pick, but sometimes he surprises me.

"DUKTIG tea set," I said—it's a real china tea set for kids, in pretty shades of blue and pink and yellow—and Walter said, "Me too." Ikea writes all the Swedish names in block caps, which is how I picture them, even when we're just saying them out loud.

"ARVIKA swivel chair," Walter said. I squinted at the page—the tall black chair that looked a little like you'd be buckled into it at a fair ride—and said, "Same."

"GULÖRT rug," I said, and pointed to the red-and-white rug with the cute owl on it. "I mean, duh."

"Not me," Walter said. "I'm STOCKHOLM sofa." He pointed to a green velvet couch.

"Seriously? The green couch?" Occasionally, Walter is a mystery to me.

"I really want a new couch," Walter said. "Zeke totally trashed ours—it's covered in something sticky that I don't really want to think about. Plus, it's not even comfortable anymore." He stuffed a handful of popcorn in his mouth. "Are the parents going to let us sit on all the couches when we go, or are they going to rush us, do you think?"

This was a good question. Walter and I prefer not to be rushed at Ikea. Every showroom is like a perfect fake room pulled out of a perfect fake house. Like a life-size diorama of the idea of living somewhere stylish. So there's the part where it's all the couches or coffee tables or whatever in one place, but there's also that same couch in a little movie-set kind of area, with a carpet, and a coffee table that has some books and magazines on it, maybe glasses on a tray, a plant, even.

Have you ever watched any of those TV shows about people living in tiny houses? I love those shows—all the people playing guitars in their perfect tiny lofts, sitting with glasses of iced tea in their perfect tiny living rooms, life miniaturized down to a manageable level. It's like my little-kid fantasy of living in my own dollhouse, using all the little accessories, the house aglow with twinkle lights, and none of the clutter of real life. Ikea felt like that to me too. Like living in a life-size dollhouse. But a really modern one, with dark wood floors and tiled bathrooms.

The one time Walter and I actually got to go to Ikea together, it was epic. We planned for it, made lists, and sat around with the catalog for weeks beforehand, daydreaming about . . . I'm not sure what. Having nicer beds, maybe, or bedrooms. Or nicer houses. Or something else. Nicer lives? I'm really not sure—except that it seems to have involved the word *nicer*. Walter and I sat in all the little rooms and pretended we lived there. We pretended to watch the TV, pretended to channel-surf with the remote control, pretended to brush our teeth in the little demo bathroom, pretended to sit at the breakfast bar and wait for pancakes. We liked to spin in all the desk chairs, and lie on all the beds, and click on all the lamps.

I'm sure I don't need to tell you that this is not how our parents like to shop. Someone kept circling back to get us. Usually my mom. The same mom who once, after we'd spent hours at Ikea picking out stuff and finding it in the warehouse and standing in line with our giant shopping cart crammed with all the boxes that contained all the parts of the sofa we were buying and also some holiday napkins and a one-dollar set of colored markers and every other thing we'd managed to load in, sighed and said, "Let's just forget it. I mean, do we even really need any of this?" And then she said, a little louder, pushing her hair out of her face in a kind of insane way, "Let's just go. Okay? Let's *go!*" And my dad recommended that she take a deep breath and go get a cup of coffee and wait in the car. Which is what she did, and she was sitting there, laughing at herself, when we came out with all the stuff.

Anyway, were the parents going to rush us? Yes. They were going to rush us. "I wish we could spend the night there," Walter said. He'd closed his eyes in the sunshine and was dreamily scratching at his Lego robotics T-shirt from the year that our team went to the state championship. "Wouldn't it be great? Like in *From the Mixed-Up Files of Mrs. Basil E. Frankweiler.*"

I knew exactly what he was talking about, because that book was one of our favorites. It's the one where a brother and sister spend a bunch of nights in the Metropolitan Museum of Art in New York City. They sleep in the antique beds and fish coins out of the fountains to buy food, and it's so awesome. It's not like one of those spend-the-night-at-the-aquarium events, where you're there with your class and a sleeping bag. I mean, I'm sure I'd love that too, but there's something so much cooler about it being secret and even kind of wrong, about nobody knowing where you are. In the book, the kids end up staying there for, like, a week, and they solve a mystery and catch a criminal and rescue a Michelangelo sculpture and do all this other stuff. But honestly? The part that always interested me most was just the actual living in the museum—the day-to-day descriptions of what they ate and where they slept and the fun things they thought to do, alone in a giant museum with no grown-ups.

"We could, you know," I said.

Walter laughed.

"I'm serious," I said. "I mean, at least kind of." I was looking up into the maple branches, scrunching my eyes half-shut to make halos around all the bright green leaves. Couldn't we? Just for one night?

"No," Walter said, because either I'd asked it out loud or he knew what I was thinking. "Impossible. First of all, because we'd never get away with it. And second of all, because the parents would go completely crazy." One time Walter and I had walked into town without leaving a note, and, as my mom likes to say, they'd practically called out the National Guard. And we were gone for, like, five minutes.

"We could," I said again, propping myself up on an

elbow to look at Walter, who was staring up into the tree.

"That would be so cool," he said. "But, Frankie? What part of *impossible* are you not getting?" He closed his eyes, in a way that was not exactly an invitation for me to keep talking.

"I'm not sure," I said quietly. "But it's true that there is some part of *impossible* that I seem to be not getting."

But what I really wanted to say was this: What part of *Walter* are you not *being*? Because this person, this hesitating, unenthusiastic person, was not my Walter. You know how I said that Walter is only occasionally a mystery to me? That used to be completely true, but now it was only a mix of true and not true. Because for the past six months, since the thing we weren't talking about, Walter had been disappearing. Or maybe *fading* is a better word, like a cutout construction-paper heart taped up on a second-grade window, getting bleached by the sun. He was still completely familiar. I mean, we still finished each other's sentences and spent almost all our time together. But there was a kind of essential Walterness that I was missing. This person shrugged and nodded or shook his head gently instead of saying "Awesome!" or "No way, no how!" the way he always had.

When Mrs. Williams, our second-grade teacher, finally took down those valentines from the window, I peeled the tape from their edges, and the color was still bright beneath it. I was thinking about that. Not about the construction paper and the tape, exactly. But about how to get the brightness back. I mean, it's not like I thought that spending the night in Ikea would be a way to do that. . . .

Actually, that's not true. That's exactly what I was starting to think.

Walter sighed then. If a picture is worth a thousand words, a sigh is worth at least a hundred. He sat up. He was pretty much done with this conversation. And yet for me, a random, crazy idea was starting to seem like the solution to everything—like the rope that would pull Walter up and out, back to me. I couldn't let it go.

"Couldn't we get away with it if the parents didn't actually know where we were?" I said, and Walter was quiet, slowly poking the end of one of his shoelaces into each of the shoelace holes in his sneakers, one at a time. *Aglet.* That's what the plasticky end of a shoelace is called. The word floated into my head, and I practically grabbed the lace out of Walter's hand. *Knock knock, hello? Anybody home?*

But then, after maybe a full minute, he said, "The big sleepover switcheroo." So I knew he knew what I was thinking. And when he smiled and opened his eyes? They were so dark they were almost black—and, finally, they were sparkling.

3

Walter

I swallowed a marble when I was two, and I can remember the cold weight of it dropping into my stomach, like a smooth, heavy secret. (Apparently, it was only a secret until my mom found it in my diaper the next day.) I'm telling you this because it's the single clear memory I have from before I met Walter. That's how long we've known each other.

Walter and I went to the same preschool, and there was a huge old pee-smelling pink couch wedged into one side of the room. It was called the "cozy corner," and you could take a book or a stuffed animal and go hang out there if you were feeling sad or shy or lazy.

Which, it turns out, Walter and I usually were—shy and lazy, at least.

"I think I have a best friend," I said to my parents one day at the dinner table. "A really, really good, nice friend," I added, and my mom and dad smiled and asked me to tell them about my new nice friend. We were probably eating mac and cheese that my mom had snuck mashed sweet potato into. "Well," I said—and this is the part of the story we've all told and retold a million times—"his name is Walter. He's got curly, curly hair. We sit on the couch together. We haven't talked to each other yet, but he's really, really, really nice."

"That sounds like a really good, nice friend," my mom said.

Of course, what we didn't know at the time was that Walter's family was having almost the exact same conversation at their house—even down to the curly, curly hair. My mom's confessed to me since then that at some point she and Alice met at a school auction committee meeting, and Mom said, "Wait, are you Walter's mom? My daughter Frankie's good-good-nice friend she's never spoken to?" And they laughed and laughed.

I totally see why it was funny. But also, we were

completely right about each other. I don't know how, but we were. The feeling I had sitting next to him on that gross old couch—the feeling that there was this warm, nice person beside me—has never really gone away. We even still sit together quietly sometimes, reading books on his couch or mine, like we did when we were three. We're like a brother and sister, is what people tell us, only I think siblings annoy each other more. I mean, I wouldn't know, since I don't have one. But it's not like we really ever drive each other crazy.

The worst argument I can remember having was the year I read the Narnia books and wanted everyone to think—and *say*—that I was a lion. I wore my lion T-shirt every day, and studied Mr. Pockets and copied how he acted, and let my hair grow into a curly yellow mane. I purred and rolled on my back and rubbed the side of my face against everyone. "Do you?" I asked Walter once. "Do you believe that I am really a real lion?" He looked at me very directly and evenly, like he does, and he said, "I know that you love lions so much, Frankie, and I believe that you really feel like a real lion." I crossed my arms and roared, and huffed out of the room in my lion T-shirt, and huffed back in to say,

"Well, you're wrong. I really am one." And Walter nodded and patted the spot next to him on the couch so we could go back to looking at the *Guinness World Records* book together. So we could look for the millionth time at the man with the crazy spiraling fingernails.

Which we did.

He's hard to describe, Walter, because he's kind of bubbling over with energy, but then he's also so chill. And some people assume he's going to be good at sports because he's black—or his mom is, so technically he's mixed race—and he's, um, *not* good at sports. One of our favorite things (it's still magneted to Walter's refrigerator) is this end-of-year report he got from our gym teacher when we were in first grade. We loved this teacher, who wrote on Walter's report: "Walter is one of the finest students I have had the pleasure of teaching. He's a model of sportsmanship, good nature, and serious effort. That said, his athletic skills will continue to develop as he works on the following:"—we especially love that colon—"Running. Jumping. Throwing balls. Catching balls. Passing. Receiving. Strength. Coordination. Balance."

Being Walter's best friend feels like cheating, in a

way, because he's so incredibly easy to get along with. If you're writing down the classmates you'd be happiest to sit next to on the field-trip bus, everyone in class writes down Walter as, at least, their second choice, if not their first. He's not hyper, but he's enthusiastic—the kind of person who says "Totally!" and "Let's!" and "Oh my god, YES!" about everything.

Or I should say *said*—because this faded Walter was more likely to shrug and say "Sure" or, worse, "Nah. I should probably think about going home pretty soon." He had even, when I told him a story about a boy interrupting me in class to miscorrect me about a Civil War fact, said mildly, "Oh well." "'Oh well'?!" I said back to him, indignant. "Walter! This kid was confusing Union and Confederate and *correcting* me!" "That sounds super annoying," Walter had said, studying the broken zipper on his hoodie, and I had let it go. I mean, he was technically saying the right things, doing the right things. But something was missing. Like his head-thrown-back laughter, which he was definitely not doing now.

What I'm trying to tell you is that I'd lost something. And I was really counting on getting it back.

4

The Not-Mystery of the Missing Doorknob

If you'd have seen me that Friday, you would have thought that I was just this normal kid doing normal stuff in a normal way. You would not have known, from looking at me, that my brain was churning ideas around like a washing machine, all suds and froth and crazy agitation. You would not have known that I was completely faking it—pretending to be in my regular body at the regular table while my mind was doing a million other things.

"Frankie, honey, can I interest you in some more

salad?" This was another recipe my mom was testing: a holiday spinach-and-cranberry something that had some kind of sweet dressing and was completely delicious. "We might as well finish it. It's not going to keep."

And I said, "Sure," and thought about how weird it is that parents can know you so totally well but also not at all. I mean, my parents are pretty great by almost any reasonable standards. Yes, sometimes I'm embarrassed when my mom comes to volunteer at school and asks all the kids a million questions about their deepest thoughts and desires. "Well, what do you think love even *means*?" she might ask someone, even though all we're doing is taping together doily-and-construction-paper valentines for our classmates. "Mom!" I say, and she says, "What? People like to be asked about themselves." And this is, I have to admit, kind of true. Everybody tells her everything. Me too—I tell her everything. Or did. Almost. Not that I always wanted to.

And now, in sixth grade? I was starting to realize that I didn't *have* to. That I could have this private part of my life inside my own head, and I could share it or not. And if I didn't, nobody would even know about it. It was kind of strange—like discovering that there was a hole in the floor underneath your bed, filled with jewels and gold coins, and you could just go ahead and not mention it to anybody.

Or like there was a secret door, and if I clicked it behind me, then it was just me alone, in my room. Oh, wait, I wouldn't know about that because . . . the door to my room didn't actually shut. Seriously. I mean, I had a door—"the nicest door in the whole house," my mom liked to say, running her hand across it tenderly, and it really was. It's made of a kind of wood called "heart pine," which I love the sound of—I picture a red valentine in the middle of a gigantic tree—and it's "original to the house," the real estate agent told us, which means that it was part of the house when it was first built, over a hundred years ago. It's gleaming and honey-colored and always seems like it's practically lit from within—you'd totally think "magic portal" if you saw it. But *it had no doorknob.*

"Someone must have thought the wood was too beautiful to mess up with hardware," my dad said when we first moved into the house. Plus, my room is so small that we're probably the first family to use it as an actual bedroom. It was probably mostly used as a storage area, even though it has the nicest window that looks out over the dogwoods and lilacs. Which was great, it really was, and it's not like there was anything in particular I wanted to do behind a closed door, but still. Sometimes I wanted privacy, just for the sake of having privacy. And to close the door at all, I had to reach around the outside and kind of pull it toward myself, so I usually ended up closing my hand in it, or pinching one of my fingers.

And even then it didn't ever really matter because a minute later one of my parents would just pull it open and come in anyway. So, yes, I wanted a doorknob. A little thing, I know. But I always worried that asking for one would be a *big* thing. I worried that it would hurt my parents' feelings, because it's just the three of us. We're such a small team, you know?

You're thinking, *Just get a doorknob at Ikea!* And that would have been a much simpler plan. I mean, it's not like Walter and I needed to spend the night there for it. But somehow the two things got blurred together in my head—wanting the apartness of a closed door, of a secret plan.

So I was there at the table, with my growing secret, and my mom was talking to my dad about the salad—"I feel like if I add poppy seeds to the dressing, it's going to turn into a cliché"—and my dad was nodding but also looking out the open window at the lilacs that were starting to turn from purple to brown, so perfumy now that it was actually kind of too much.

And I was thinking that if I didn't talk about Ikea at all, that would be so unlike me that they'd get suspicious. Which is crazy, really. What would they suspect me of? Plotting to spend the night in a gigantic Swedish warehouse store? That really doesn't seem like it would be high on their list of things to worry about. But I was still kind of paranoid, so I said, "I'm really excited about Ikea!" only it came out of my mouth so oddly—like I was a croaking frog crossed with an excited preschooler—that both of my parents turned to look at me.

"You're really excited about Ikea!" my dad said, the way you'd talk to a croaking-frog-preschooler, and I laughed.

"I just am is all," I said, lamely. And my mom smoothed my hair off my forehead and said, "We know you are, sweetie," like I was four.

Later, after we'd cleared the dinner dishes from the table, after we'd evaluated my mom's pumpkin whoopee pies (tasty), after we'd watched a reality show about people looking to move into, yes, a tiny house ("I'm not watching this crap," my mom always says, before she settles into the couch between Dad and me and watches with us), after we talked about how hilarious it is that the people are always appalled by how small the tiny houses are ("Isn't that kind of the whole premise of the show?" my mom asked, and my dad said, imitating one of the house-hunters, "But where will I put my grand piano?"), and after I kissed my parents good night, I finally climbed into bed with Mr. Pockets and my own excitement.

It felt like the night before Christmas—the way you keep telling yourself that if you just close your eyes and go to sleep, then it will feel like it's morning the very next second. This worked about as well as it does on Christmas Eve—which is to say, not at all. And it was not visions of sugarplums. It was visions of doorknobs. A whole Ikea wall of them. It was visions of Walter, his eyes scrunched up with laughter, like they were supposed to be. It was visions of me, doing this crazy thing with him that would be ours and only ours.

"What's the thing you're most scared of?" I had asked Walter at lunch earlier that day. We were sitting outside with our backs against the sun-warmed brick school building, sharing the end of a bag of vending-machine potato chips.

"In general?" Walter said, and he looked alarmed. "You mean, like, snakes, heights, the infiniteness of the universe?"

"No, silly. About Ikea."

"I don't know," Walter said quickly, squinting a little in the sunshine. "What about for you?"

"Oh, I guess the obvious," I said. "That my parents will find out and be angry. Or worse than angry. *Disappointed* in me."

"Then why are you even running away?" Walter said.

I turned to look at him. Now I was confused. "I'm not," I said. "We're not running *away*. We're running *to* Ikea! Because it's going to be awesome!"

Walter nodded.

"So, what about you?" I said. "What are you scared of?"

And he said, totally vaguely, "Same."

"Same what?"

"Same as you, I guess," he said, and before I could even look into his face to try to understand anything, he stood up, brushed the sour-cream-and-onion crumbs from his jeans, and headed for the door.

After school, we'd gone to Walter's house to make packing lists and rehearse the parent conversations, practicing for different scenarios, in case talking to them didn't go as smoothly as we hoped it would. We'd even decided on a cancel-mission code phrase, to use in the event things were going badly. (It was, maybe ironically, "mixed-up files.") When I was getting on my bike to go home, I'd blurted out, "What are you looking forward to the most?" Walter was standing in his doorway, and he furrowed his brow and shrugged, said, "Ikea." I put my feet back on the ground and looked hard at him. "You're in, right?" And he nodded, not smiling, and said, "I'm in." Then he put his hand up in a wave and disappeared into the house.

I was thinking about this now, in bed. We *weren't* running from anywhere, were we? Walter and I? It was Ikea itself that had us so crazily excited. At least I thought it was. Even though I turned out to be wrong about this, like I turned out to be wrong about so many things.

Shhh, I thought at my brain, because I was never going to get any sleep with it making so much noise.

But there was no shushing it, and I lay on my back in the dark with Mr. Pockets on my chest, stroking his sleeping cheeks, listening to my heartbeat echoing up through the pillow, smelling the lilacs blowing in. I was wondering if Walter was lying awake at his house, and thinking that he probably was. Or at least hoping.

5

And So It Begins

"Wait, what's that for?" my mom asked. It was, finally, Saturday afternoon. We were in the driveway, and I had my old blue Dora the Explorer backpack on—the one I used to love because it was so awesome, but that I loved now because it was so corny.

"My overnight stuff."

"Wait," my mom said. "Isn't Walter coming *here* after?"

"No, no," I said, the lie catching in my throat. "*I'm* going *there*."

My mom shrugged, nodded. "Okay. Whatever you guys want, as long as it's okay with Alice."

If everything was going according to plan, then right about now Walter was having the exact same conversation with his mom. I pictured Alice shrugging just like my mom had. I could practically hear her say, "As long as it's good with Frankie's mom and dad."

I climbed into the back of the blue Subaru and buckled up, and my dad asked if I wanted to listen to an audiobook or a podcast or anything, and I said, "Nah, I'm good," distracted. My mom had already started the engine, but she turned around to put her palm on my forehead. "What?" I said, and she said, "Oh, you know, you turned down the chance to listen to a book, so I'm just making sure you don't have a fever." "Ha-ha," I said, and then rested my head against the cool window while the scenery scrolled past: first our neighborhood, with all its little houses; then the bigger houses; then our school, the town hall where the farmers' market is, the shops and bakeries on Main Street; and, eventually, the boring highway. I was imagining being in Ikea with just Walter, and in my mind it was kind of like that scene from *Charlie and the Chocolate Factory* where they get to the meadow and everything is made of candy: the daffodils, the toadstools, the chocolate river. Then I remembered how Augustus Gloop actually fell into that chocolate river and almost drowned. I think it's safe to say that I was having what they call "mixed emotions." Ikea's just about an hour from our house, but it felt more like five minutes before the GPS was announcing, in its automated voice, "Turn *left* on Ikea *Way*."

"Remember the first time we came here?" Dad said. "And you were like, 'Wow! *Ikea* is on *Ikea* Way! That's such a funny coincidence.'" I laughed. I did remember. Of course, how it actually works is that they build the store and then name the road after it—Ikea is so big that it changes the cartography of the region where they build it—but I didn't realize it at the time.

Ikea, I happen to know, because I am obsessed with it, was started in Sweden in 1943 by a *seventeen-year-old*. Ingvar Kamprad, who was, in case you missed it in the last sentence, *seventeen*! And now it is the world's largest furniture seller. There are 389 stores in 48 countries, and a few years ago, Ingvar Kamprad was listed as one of the world's richest people. From the company he started when he was *seventeen*. That makes me feel like I've got about five years to figure out something really great to do.

The big blue-and-yellow Ikea signs were coming

into view, and my mom was squinting at them, trying to figure out which way to turn. "*Overnight* parking?" she said, and my dad laughed.

"Over*height* parking," he said. "Like, for big, tall trucks. But it *is* funny to imagine spending the night here. You could sleep in one of the showrooms, help yourself to the meatballs!" My dad laughed again, but I couldn't even pretend to. I mean, I think my heart literally stopped beating. "Right, Frank?" he said, and turned around to smile at me, and I tried to smile back and made a sound—"Ha! Ha!"—like a robot laughing. My dad raised his eyebrows at my weirdness and turned back to the parking situation.

"Where are we meeting those guys again?" my mom asked as she turned into a narrow spot. "Couches," I said. "We figured it would be a comfy place to wait if someone was late."

"Good thinking!" Mom said, and smiled at me in the rearview mirror.

We walked across the parking lot and through those big automatic doors, and the world opened up into huge spaces and metal ductwork in the ceiling and total *newness*. The wonderful, amazing Ikea smell was everywhere: wood and cinnamon, potted ferns and coffee, and something that's probably chemicals. "Smell that!" I said, inhaling happily. "That's the Ikea smell!" My dad smiled and patted me, then made the twirly-finger cuckoo gesture next to his head, which made me laugh.

We took the escalator up to the showrooms, wound our way through the life-size dioramas of kitchens and dining rooms, and arrived in the sofa section, where, sure enough, Walter and his mom were sitting together on a green velvet couch—the one Walter had picked from the catalog—like they were home watching a movie. Zeke was running in a huge spiral on a carpet with a huge spiral pattern on it.

Walter smiled when he saw us, and Alice stood up to kiss us all. I said hi to Zeke, who was starting another spiral and couldn't stop to greet us. "Zeke, honey, please," Alice said. "I'm getting dizzy." Zeke stopped short, flapped his arms around for a second, and then fell over. We heard his voice say, from the carpet, "Me too."

I saw immediately that Walter had his backpack. He was in. He was with me. I'd doubted him, but here he was.

Alice gathered Zeke up, then stood and gestured to

my backpack. "Isn't Walter going to your house after?" she said.

"I actually thought Frankie was going to *your* house after," my mom said.

"Oh, sure," Alice said. "She's welcome to."

"Perfect," my mom said. "Either way is great with us. We can just figure it out later."

"Or they could just stay here," my dad said, and the grown-ups laughed. My own personal heart stopped beating for the second time in ten minutes. Walter and I did not look at each other. Well, I don't know what he was looking at, since I didn't look at him. But I'm guessing it was anything but me.

6

Shoppers and Spies

We were eager to check out our favorite spots, but the parents had to stop in the entryway area to study various boring pieces of mudroom furniture. Zeke wedged himself into a boot drawer, and when I saw him, he put a finger to his lips in that adorable, exaggerated toddler *shhh* sign. Then he said loudly, "I'm hiding."

"If only we could find Zeke!" my dad said, and Zeke laughed, because he's easy like that.

The adults were talking about shoes, surreptitiously removing their own to see how many pairs this or that bench could hold.

Once Walter's mom had figured out which model

she was buying, she wrote down the number and name and color with the little stub pencil so that she could find the right flat-pack boxes later, in the floor-to-ceiling stacks of boxes in the warehouse. "Or, you know, *not* find them," Alice said, laughing. "Which is much more likely."

You have to find everything yourself, cram it into your car, then screw everything together at home. It's like a grown-up version of a make-your-own solar-powered car kit.

Walter and I wandered away to sit on a couch and whisper about our plans for later. And, honestly? I'm practically too embarrassed to even tell you about them. They were so boring. You'd think that we'd be plotting all kinds of crazy stuff. I mean, a giant warehouse all to ourselves! Right? But really we were just thinking about all the new furniture we wanted to sit on, lie on, all the stylish or cozy places where we wanted to curl up and relax. We were not exactly criminal masterminds.

And, of course, because we're like weird Ikea detectives, we ended up eavesdropping on some of the other shoppers. "Sure," one man was saying, though you didn't actually get a *sure* vibe off him. His face was very red, and the woman he was with had her mouth arranged in a short, straight line. "But what we're really going to need—if you're getting all this crap—is a bigger *home*." Walter raised his eyebrows in a kind of exaggerated grimace. Kids love Ikea, but we'd noticed that it makes grown-ups want to kill each other. It's like they want all the stuff, but then they really kind of hate it too.

Walter got up to look at an odd wicker chaise lounge, which he lay down on. "This is not a comfortable piece of furniture," he said. He closed his eyes, then snapped them open again. "Did you sleep much last night?" he said. And I said, "Oh, totally! For at least a single minute."

Walter laughed. "Same. It was like the night before Christmas. Or Hanukkah. Or something."

"I know exactly what you mean," I said.

Then Walter shushed me and sat up.

"Kids." My dad had come up behind us. "We were thinking about getting some dinner. Are you guys hungry?" We were. We were starving. Dad sat down on a wicker armchair, said, "Youch," and then, "Hey, isn't Zeke with you?" and I seriously thought he was kidding, until we said no. Dad stood up quickly then and said, "Uh-oh. Walter, let's find your mom." We stood up too, and we all began retracing our steps, winding through the other shoppers and calling for Zeke in a semi-loud voice—loud enough so he could hopefully hear us, but not loud enough to cause an all-out store panic. Not yet, at least.

We found the moms, and we all split up to look for Zeke, peeking into chairs and beds, trying to imagine where you would go if you were a very small boy. The kids' area seemed like an obvious choice, but it was pretty far from where we'd gotten to. Was he hiding in another drawer? A cabinet? We opened them all, calling softly. "Zeee-keee! Come out, come out, wherever you are!"

Walter's mom briefly freaked out at the idea that he had climbed into one of the refrigerators and was suffocating, but they turned out to have special suffocation preventers that kept the doors from sealing all the way. One fridge did have a humongous freezer drawer that I looked in, but there was just some baby's old pacifier in it. No Zeke.

Walter heard him first. He stopped, put a finger to his lips. "Listen," he said, and I heard it too.

"Waltie! Mommy! I'm here! I'm fine! I'm almost done!"

Walter furrowed his eyebrows questioningly at me, and I shrugged. "Zekey-Deke," Walter called again. "Where are you?"

"Here!" Zeke called, and we were definitely getting closer. "In here! Almost done! But they're out of toilet paper. Can you get me some?"

Walter said, "Oh my god," and his mom, who had caught up with us, slapped her hand to her forehead.

"I can't look," she said, and we were all laughing already, shaking our heads and laughing and saying, "Oh no. Oh no."

We peered around a pretend doorway, into a showroom bathroom, and Zeke cried out, "You found me!" He was sitting on the toilet with his pants and undies scrunched down around his ankles. There was a bad smell. "Mommy!" he said. "Can you please get the toilet paper? I turded out a ginormous *turd*!" Walter's mom had her hand over her mouth and was shaking her head, laughing completely silently. "All by my own self, Mommy! In the big-boy potty. Can we ride the escalator again?"

It could have been worse. Yes, the other customers were hurrying by with their hands over their noses, peeking in and shaking their heads, but we got Zeke cleaned up without too much fuss. ("Thank goodness for this handy-dandy package of FANTASTISK napkins!" Alice laughed.) He was totally baffled by the experience. "Why is there a toilet that's not for pooping in?" Zeke kept saying. "That's *crazy*! Right? A toilet that's not for pooping!" And the parents agreed that it was very confusing. My dad whispered to me, "Didn't we see something like that on *Jackass*? Where the guy craps in the Home Depot toilet?" And my mom just shook her head and said, "I still can't believe you let her watch that."

All things considered, the Ikea people were amazingly friendly about the whole thing. "We actually have a sign," the floor manager told us, and he pointed to a little plaque next to the toilet: CUSTOMER RESTROOMS ARE LOCATED NEXT TO THE RESTAURANT. "But honestly? There's a lot of overlap between people who use the showroom toilets and people who don't read yet."

7

Swedish Meatballs

Finding our way back to the restaurant wasn't as easy as you might think. "This place is like a *maze*," my dad complained when we got to another dead end. We could actually *see* the cafeteria. We just couldn't get to it without taking all these roundabout detours.

And Walter and I couldn't really walk past anything without doing a lot of nudging each other and pointing to things, nodding when we understood what the other person was excited about. The spinning chairs! The room full of bedding! The art supplies! The fleets of enormous couches! Our favorite showrooms! It was fun to be there with Zeke and the grown-ups, but I couldn't wait for them to leave. Also, if this makes sense, I was dreading them leaving. Like that feeling you have when you're in line for a roller coaster, dying to get to the front, but you kind of wish it would take even longer. I had butterflies in my stomach. Or something more like, maybe, *dragons* in my stomach.

"What are you two up to?" my mom said at some point. "It's like you're naughty preschoolers all over again!" Walter giggled, which made me laugh.

The cafeteria, when we finally got there, was pretty exciting just by itself. I'm not sure what it is about the food, but it is just so crazy good, you can't believe it. You can get Swedish meatballs and mashed potatoes and gravy and this yummy lingonberry sauce, all on a huge plate for cheap, and then for one more dollar, you can get five extra meatballs—which means that for two more dollars, you can get *ten* extra meatballs. "Are you going to go into one of your famous meatball comas?" my mom asked, looking at my crazy heaped-up plate, and probably yes, I was. Ikea meatballs are my favorite.

Mom once made Swedish meatballs for me at home, with that same creamy brown gravy and everything, and when I bit into one, she was looking hard at me. "How is it?" she asked. And I said, "Oh my god, so

45

good!" And she was actually mad! "I can't believe you think they're not as good as the meatballs at stupid Ikea!" she said. And I said, "I didn't say that!" And she said, "But I know it's true." Which was annoying but accurate, even though my mom is an awesome cook.

Walter evaluated the salads and took a spinach one that had strawberries and blue cheese on it. "Excuse me, Mr. Fancy," I said.

He shrugged. "Oh, sorry, did you want me to bite into a cow? Or a *horse*? Or whatever poor animal it is you're eating?" Fair enough.

Zeke was super excited about his moose-shaped pasta kid's meal. "Can I really, really get that?" he asked, then he hugged Alice's knees and said, "You're such a sweetheart," which made us laugh.

I also picked out a pear-flavored soda, which came in a big can with a green pear on it. I have a semi-secret collection of cans, which drives my parents crazy because, to quote my mom, "We barely have enough room for our stuff, let alone for your collection of actual garbage." I have a grape soda can from Japantown, and a Coke can in Arabic that a friend of my parents brought me back from Morocco, and a can from this terrible bitter soda called Moxie that we drank in Maine, and, well, lots of cans, actually. I was planning to keep this one too. "Please tell me you're not going to keep that can," my mom said now, and I shrugged and gave her my guilty smile.

A confession: the cans are not my only weird collection. In the course of my life, I have, at different moments, collected the following things: dryer lint, cat hair, bottle caps, dust (in a Flintstones vitamin jar), sawdust, rubber bands, cactuses, miniature picture frames, postcards with cats on them, and—my one normal collection—state quarters. I was also currently obsessed with a small collection of what Walter called "sad mugs." These were handmade clay mugs that we usually found at the Goodwill or garage sales and that looked like a little kid had made them in a beginner pottery class. They had drooping, lumpy handles, and they tended to be really large and really thick, glazed in various shades of brown and brownish green. They were completely *not* Ikea, and they totally broke my heart.

We sat at one of the high tables by a window, the kind that has the tall clear-red stools that I love. The sky was starting to fade a little, and the twinkle lights strung above us looked so pretty. A Swedish flag flapped a little in the breeze outside. The meatballs were peppery and good, and I spaced out happily, not really listening to the grown-ups, who were talking about the lighting and what exactly made it so perfect, which got them to talking about Ikea and what exactly made it so popular.

"One in three Europeans is conceived on an Ikea bed," Walter announced. "I read it in my *Book of Useful Information*."

"What's *conceive*?" Zeke asked. And Alice immediately said, "It means *have an idea*."

"That makes sense," Zeke said. "I have *lots* of ideas in bed."

Walter smiled at me quickly, before Zeke could see.

It was comfortable there, and I relaxed a little. We talked some and spied some more on other people's conversations. A couple crept slowly by us, talking too quietly for us to hear. The woman had a long gray ponytail, and the man had electrical tape on the bridge of his glasses and a piece of cake on the tray that was balanced on his walker. Two forks. They were smiling.

A girl with short bleached hair and a lot of pierced things—eyebrows and ears, lip and nose—sat with her parents, looking angrily out the window. The parents were eating, nobody talking, and I felt so bad for them. Teenagers. Oof. That would be Walter and me soon. Would we be like that too? I couldn't picture it.

A baby whose bib was ecstatically covered in food was yelling. "Ya ya ya ya ya YA YA YA YA YA!" "That is a noisy baby," Zeke said, shaking his head judgmentally. "A noisy, *messy* baby." Zeke himself was covered in juice and tomato sauce, but we had the good manners not to point this out to him.

There were parents everywhere, blotting at everybody's faces with napkins, holding babies up into the air to sniff at their butts, leaning over with forks and knives to cut up everybody's food.

All these people were here at Ikea, in the middle of their own lives—each person having a particular experience of it, just like we were. You could make up stories to explain what you were seeing, but you couldn't really know, just like they couldn't know, if they looked at us, how it was we were all related or connected, or why we were there. What it was we were there to do.

At some point there was a loud barking sound, and I looked up and saw a woman a few tables away, laughing with her head thrown back and a mouthful of French fries, completely bald. My mom put a hand on Alice's shoulder, and they smiled at each other in a sad-grown-up way. "Oh, honey," my mom said, and she wrapped her arms around Alice. Alice put her head on my mom's shoulder, and I saw Walter look away.

"It could just be how she chooses to wear her hair," he said. His tight voice was uncharacteristically un-Walter-like. Usually he's so gentle. "Or, you know, wear her . . . *head*. I'm just saying everything doesn't have to be the saddest thing possible."

And his mom said, "True enough," and smiled a less sad smile at him.

Meanwhile, my dad was teaching Zeke to flip a coin, and he was getting the hang of it. "I'm unnatural!" he announced. "Head or tails!" he yelled, flipping a penny, which flew off and landed on the floor, and then, "Tails! But *why* am I unnatural?"

"*A* natural," my dad said, laughing. "It just means being good at something easily."

"I really am!" Zeke said, scrambling after the penny. "I'm *so* natural, right, Mom?"

Alice laughed and said, "The naturalest."

After we'd eaten, Alice snuck back into line and got six pieces of pink marzipan cake, which she fit together into a kind of lopsided circle, then she opened a bag

50

of squat little tea-light candles from her cart, put one on top of the sort-of cake, and lit it. We sang "Happy Birthday" and Walter blew out his candle, his eyes shut wishing-tight. Alice kissed him and said, "If your wish was a Mama kiss, it's already come true!" Walter smiled. A thread of smoke snaked up toward the ceiling, and if this had been a movie, the camera would have lingered over it in a meaningful way.

8

Mixed-Up Files

After eating is when you need to help the grown-ups rally a little, because they deflate like helium balloons, all their energy and lift gone suddenly. If they could drift down to the floor, they would. I clapped my hands. "Maybe you guys should get some coffee," I said, and the parents laughed.

"Okay, okay," my dad said. "We're on it. We're moving."

"Me too," Zeke said, and scrambled up into my lap. He put his face very close to mine and touched the groove above my lip. "This," he said, leaning in closer to whisper spittily into my ear, "is called your *philtrum.*"

Seriously, that kid knows the weirdest things. "Shhhh."
He put a finger to my lips and shook his head. "Our
little secret," I said, and he nodded and winked at me
with both eyes.

We still had the Marketplace to go through, which
is where all the little stuff is: the plates and frames and
kitchen things. It's one of my favorite parts of the store,
and I'm not even sure why. I hear myself asking if we
can get these totally random things, and I'm as mysti-
fied as my parents are. I want a multipack of tiny glass
bowls, a blue spatula, a tiered serving platter that makes
me feel like if we had one, we'd throw a tea party every
day, with cupcakes and fancy little sandwiches. "Why
do you even *want* a pair of rubber funnels?" my mom
was asking now, and I truly didn't know.

"Um, awkward," Walter said, and held them in front
of his chest like boobs, which made me laugh.

"Oooh," my mom was saying to my dad. "Ceiling
clips. We actually need these."

"What makes them ceiling clips?" I asked, and my
mom looked at me blankly.

"You know, because you can use them to close an
open bag of potato chips."

"On the *ceiling?*" I was picturing bags and bags of

chips clipped to the ceiling, but I didn't even know why you'd want that. Maybe to save space?

My mom sighed and showed me the package. "Sealing, honey. *Sealing*. With an *S*."

Oh.

Meanwhile, Walter was holding up a casserole, reading the tag. "Chafing dish?" he said. "Ew. What do you do, just kind of rub it against your thighs until you get a rash?"

"Not that kind of chafing," my mom said, "but ew."

The parents were pretty much done with Ikea now. You could see it. We were at the candle display, pillars and tapers and votives, white wax in different shapes as far as the eye could see. There was a glass lantern I had my eye on—the kind of thing you would hang on a tree over your patio and when you lit it in the evening it would make you feel instantly like you lived in a magazine. "What do you think of this?" I asked my mom, and she said, "We could get it in case we ever have a patio!"

"What time do they close?" my dad was asking, looking at his watch. Zeke was on his shoulders, slumping a little and holding two handfuls of my dad's hair like they were reins.

"I think eight," Alice said. "An hour. Here, let me take him." She reached up for Zeke. "Zekey, honey, don't pull."

Back on the floor, on his own two feet, Zeke rubbed his eyes with his fists and frowned a cartoon sad-baby frown.

"Look out," Walter whispered to me. "Possible meltdown in Zekeville. This could work well for us." I didn't know what he meant about Zeke's falling apart being a good thing, but I trusted he was right.

The store was emptying out, and the shoppers who were left seemed to be collapsing, like windup toys winding down. We saw five girls asleep on a couch in size order—the oldest was our age—and then we saw their dad gently shaking them, one at a time. "Wake up, ladies, time to go." In a flower-patterned armchair, a tiny boy in a Spider-Man costume was asleep in the lap of an old woman, who was also asleep.

"'Creatures are starting to think about rest,'" Walter said to Zeke. He was quoting *Dr. Seuss's Sleep Book*, and Zeke said back sleepily, "'Two Biffer-Baum Birds are now building their nest.'"

We headed into the warehouse to find all the things everyone was getting: the patio table (for our not-patio) and the shoe bench, packed flat in their cardboard boxes; the sofa cover; and some last-minute packages of dish towels and paper napkins. "Oh jeez," Alice was saying. "Aisle three, bin twenty-seven, what the—? I see everything but the shoe bench. I see the coatrack. The hat rack. The shoe bench? Anybody?"

My mom was looking too. "Here, here, Alice," she said, leaning in to pull a long package from the back of a shelf. "This." Alice smiled tiredly and made an exasperated sound in the back of her throat, and my mom hugged her. My dad had gotten everything we needed, and we pushed our giant ship of a cart into the line.

"These, Mama? These?" Zeke was holding out bags of little Swedish chocolate bars, bags of Swedish gummy candies, and Alice kept saying, "No, honey. No. We'll get you an ice-cream cone on the way out. No candy." "What's that cimminon smell?" Zeke said. "What is it? Is it cimminon buns? Can we get those?" Alice smiled. "Cinnamon buns. It is. Do you want that instead of an ice cream?" And Zeke pulled his eyebrows together, then shook his head. "Ice cream."

Walter and I were standing quietly together with our backpacks on. "You guys look like a criminal gang of two," my dad said cheerfully. "What exactly are you plotting?"

"As if!" I said, too loud, and Walter gave me a look. I laughed nervously out my nose, which made my dad laugh.

"Jeez," he said. "I was only kidding."

Walter dimpled his dimples at him, and my dad reached out a hand to rumple his hair.

As Walter had predicted, Zeke was quickly becoming a puddle of melting preschooler. "These, Mama? These?" He was grabbing at more and more things— cookies, licorice—pulling his eyebrows together angrily every time Alice tried to pry something out of his little fists.

"Honey, can you please take him to get an ice-cream cone?" Alice handed Walter a five-dollar bill. We took Zeke's hands, swinging him between us as we walked. "Old McDonald had a ice-cream cone," Zeke sang, while we waited in the snack line. Walter and I were playing the picking game, pointing into the refrigerator case where they sell packaged things you can take home.

"Västerbotten cheese?" I said. "Not that I know what it is."

Walter pointed and said, "This, let's see. . . . What even *is* it?" He leaned in to look at the blue metal tube. "Herring paste!" he said. "Intriguing but gross. Can I just pick chocolate?"

"And on that ice-cream cone he had a ice-cream cone!" Zeke was still singing. "With a ice-cream cone here, and a ice-cream cone there! Ha-ha, that's what I sang, right, guys? That's what I *am* singing! Right?" Walter bugged his eyes out at me, and I couldn't help laughing.

By the time Alice was done paying, we were sitting on a bench with our cones, Zeke's dripping down his shirt in vanilla swirls and smears, but he was happy. "Help me to the car, you guys, would you?" Alice said, and Walter and I grabbed the handle of the cart and pushed.

Alice was rummaging through her bag for the car keys, completely distracted as we steered the cart through the parking lot. She didn't even look up when she said, "What did you guys decide about tonight?"

Walter looked at me, his eyes wide. This was the moment. The bait and switch! We had actually practiced this very conversation. "Frankie's mom decided it would be really helpful to her if we stayed there after all," Walter said. "She's testing a bunch of brunch recipes." He paused, then added nervously, "Bunch of brunch! That's a funny rhyme. Bunch of brunch! Brunch bunch."

Luckily, Alice had her back to us. She'd found her keys and was unlocking the back of the van. I caught Walter's eye and made a finger-across-the-throat motion to get him to stop talking. "Anyways," Walter said, "I think we're going to Frankie's. I mean, I *know* we are." He really, really needed to stop talking.

I panicked then. Did Walter want to be doing this? What was the code phrase? "Mixed-up files," I said, and Alice said, "What?" and Walter said, "No. Unless they're *your* mixed-up files, Frankie."

"They're not," I said. And Alice said, "Um, right," her head in the car. "Okay. Let me know if we're ever having a planet-earth kind of conversation."

"Mixed-up files!" Zeke yelled, and I laughed.

"It's probably just as well you're not coming home with me," Alice said, "since Tired McFussypants could probably use a little one-on-one time. Right, Tired?"

"I'm fuzzy but not tired," Zeke said, yawning, and he put his arms out to get picked up. Alice buckled him into his car seat.

Walter was squatting in the back of the van, and I was trying to pass him the boxes, even though some of them were really heavy. "Here, let me." Alice took the other end of one and said, "Frankie! My gosh. Your arms are shaking. Take a break for a second."

My arms *were* shaking. "Oh, I'm just nervous because your son and I are about to go back into Ikea and spend the night there illegally by ourselves," I didn't say. I just said, "I know! I know. It's so weird. Isn't it so weird? How your arms shake? And you're like, *Oh my gosh, my arms are totally shaking!*"

Now it was Walter's turn to look at me, to shake his head. I fake-slapped my own forehead and stopped talking. Walter climbed back out of the van, and Alice slammed it shut.

"Okeydoke, kiddos. Call me in the morning, will you, honey?" She looked at him for a second. "Are you sure you and Frankie don't want to come home with us? I'm going to miss you! Okay, okay. I know. I love you. Have so much fun." She kissed Walter and kissed me, and we leaned in to say good-bye to Zeke before sliding the back door closed. "Thanks for all your help, you guys! Oh, Frankie, please thank your parents for me. I didn't even really say good-bye to them."

She started to drive off, then stopped short, and the passenger-side window rolled down. Alice leaned over to yell something at us. "Walter! Oh my god! We didn't get your desk chair!" She honestly looked like she was going to cry.

"I totally don't care, Mom," Walter said quickly. "Now we've got an excuse to come back! We'll get it next time."

Alice shook her head and blew him a kiss. "Walter. You're the best! Love you guys!"

"Love you guys," we heard Zeke echo from the back.

We waved as they drove off, doing our best impression of normal kids about to have a sleepover. Then Walter grabbed my arm, tipped his face up toward the sky, and made a crazy yelling sound in the back of his throat. "Hyperventilating!" he said. And I said, "Seriously?" And he said, "No! But I'm kind of freaking out."

"Me too," I said. "But, Walter? If we're doing this? If we really are? We've got to run back and say good-bye to my parents before they figure out that your mom's not still here."

"We're really doing this," he said, and held up his fist, which I awkwardly bumped with my own.

We ran back into the store just as my parents were

finishing paying. "Mom, Dad, we gotta run! Alice is pulling the car around and Zeke's falling apart!"

"Oh, okay," my mom said. "So you're going there? That's good. That's nice for Alice. We can do the waffles another time. Come next weekend, Walter—can you?"

Walter nodded, and my dad kissed me and said, "Call us in the morning?" and I said I would.

Walter and I ran back out the automatic sliding doors and didn't stop running until we'd rounded the corner away from the main parking lot and were completely, definitely out of sight.

9

Plan B

Walter and I stopped running and stood with our hands on our thighs, panting. Walter squeezed his side with his hand—"Cramp!"—then raised his eyebrows like, *Now what?* We'd been so focused on getting through the parent part that we hadn't finished deciding what we were going to do next. I looked at my watch.

"Let's see," I said. "The store closes in about twenty minutes. Should we go with plan A?" We needed to find somewhere to wait while the store finished closing—somewhere to hide while the cleaning crews came through, or the restocking people, or whatever happened in the time after the store closed. Plan A was hiding in the bathroom, like the *Basil E. Frankweiler* kids do. I imagined the scene like in the book, sitting on top of the toilets with our legs pulled up so nobody could see our feet dangling below.

Walter nodded. "Yup," he said. "Plan A." He grabbed my arm and we started running the way we'd come.

But just as we turned back toward the entrance, I saw the Subaru. I stopped short and grabbed Walter's hand, and he said, "What—?" but then he saw it too. We flattened ourselves against the building, breathless, and watched my mom and dad wrangling a large rectangular box onto the roof of the car with a bungee cord. They were maybe fifty yards from us. Walter grabbed my arm and pulled me back behind the building, and we squatted down. "That was a close one!" Walter said, like we were in a movie, and I said, "Seriously."

We waited a few minutes, mostly just watching the second hand on Walter's watch, but at some point he said to me, "Are you sure you want to do this? Because we could still totally catch up to your parents, if you'd rather."

I pictured the huge open cube of the store, full of all the fun we were planning to have. I pictured my door at home, without its doorknob. I pictured Walter picturing . . . okay, I couldn't actually picture what Walter was picturing.

And I said, "I do want to." Because I did. Or at least I mostly did. But I added, "Same for you. It's fine if you're changing your mind. You know I'd understand a hundred percent."

He shook his head. "Now that we're doing this, I almost feel like I *need* to do this, if that makes any sense." It did. Or it mostly did. Actually, I'm not sure if I knew what he meant, but I nodded.

Walter and I had once come up with an elaborate plan to have Puddle and Mr. Pockets meet. We were going to smuggle them out in their carrying cases and meet halfway between our houses, where we were going to take the cats out of their cases and hold them up, nose to nose, so they could know each other even just a little bit. "So *that's* who I've been smelling," we imagined them saying to themselves, after years of sniffing us when we got home from each other's houses. Only when the time came to put Mr. Pockets in his carrier, I chickened out. I was so worried that he would get out, that he would get lost and be lost forever, and it would all be because of this stupid plan that wasn't even really important. So I ran empty-handed to the meeting place, and there was Walter, running from the opposite direction, catless too, for the same reason.

In other words, we had a history of chickening out.

"Do you think the coast is clear?" I said, and Walter smiled and said, "How come every single thing either one of us says sounds like a line from *Scooby-Doo*?" It was true. It really was that kind of plan, with a funny cartoon feeling to it. We decided the coast *was* clear, and we turned back around and walked in through the automatic doors and headed up the escalator. The store was mostly emptied out, and I felt like everyone was looking at us suspiciously, even though I knew they probably really weren't.

Probably they were just thinking that the store was about to close and that they were never going to fit all the giant boxes in the car. Or they were thinking about how, once they got home, they were going to fight while they tried to follow the crazily confusing instructions for assembling their new furniture. At my own house, my dad would notice that there was one screw missing out of the thousand they needed to put together whatever they were putting together, and my mom would shake her head, drop it into her hands, mumble a long line of swear words. I was happy not to be hearing that.

While Walter and I were walking purposefully through the store, we talked out the sides of our mouths, looking straight ahead. "Bathroom on the main floor or the lower level?" Walter asked sideways, and I answered sideways, "Main floor."

When we got to the bathrooms, there was nobody coming out of or going into them. The doors had stick-figure pictures on them: one with legs, one with a tri-angle. Pants, I guess, and a skirt. "I bet you love that," Walter teased, pointing at them. I was kind of notori-ous for hating gender stereotypes.

"Oh, I do," I said. "Hang on. Let me tape a triangle to my waist so I know which bathroom to use." I'd re-cently seen someone add details to an image like this—they'd drawn in the legs and sides of the body—so that instead of a skirt, it was clear that what the figure was wearing was actually a superhero cape flowing down around them. I loved that.

We heard the crazy-loud hand dryer go off inside, and a woman straggled out, looking dazed. "Ikea zom-bie," Walter observed, and I realized we were stalling.

"Maybe we don't have to hide in the bathrooms," I said. "I mean, there have got to be a million better and, you know, less gross places to hide, right? Did we have a plan B?"

"What about that loft bed in that one showroom?" Walter said. "The one with the pink everything? That was plan B. At least it is now." Perfect. We turned back the way we had come, and headed for the showrooms.

Once we arrived at the pink-everything loft bed, Walter grabbed my hand, then looked both ways before climbing the ladder. I did the same, and we found ourselves in a cozy nook beneath the pretend ceiling— a wooden platform filled with deep pink pillows and comforters, everything so fresh and new-smelling. A voice over the loudspeaker announced fifteen minutes to closing, and Walter and I looked at each other and shook our heads, smiling. *We were doing this.* And it was already perfect. It was already just so completely perfect.

10

The Kind of Kids We Are

We didn't really know how long it would take for the store to close or what would happen afterward. Were there security guards all over the place? Did they turn the lights off? Would there be a million people everywhere, cleaning and restocking? We had no idea. We peeked out from our nest every minute or so, and we could see various last-licks shoppers hurrying toward the exits, a couple of Ikea workers rushing by with their phones pressed to their ears. Meanwhile, Walter and I were unzipping our backpacks to show each other what we'd brought, organizing everything on top of the flower-patterned comforter. The whole night stretched out before us like a deserted beach—wide open, full of possibility, and maybe, I admit, a little lonely.

"Empty soda can, very useful," Walter teased when I pulled it out. I had, indeed, taken it from dinner. We were talking quietly, hoping our voices were muffled by all the bedding.

"Smart," I said when he showed me *From the Mixed-Up Files*. "For research. And moral support."

"Good thinking," he said when I showed him that I'd brought the Ikea catalog. I'd also brought playing cards and a camera. Walter had brought binoculars and a first-aid kit that appeared to be just three Band-Aids inside an Altoids tin. I'd brought my Swiss Army knife. Walter had brought the walkie-talkies we'd discussed in our planning stages. (Neither of us had a cell phone.) I took one of them now and put it in my backpack, and he nodded.

We'd both packed notebooks and pens, headlamps, and water bottles. Walter teased that we were the kind of kids who would row away to a deserted island having brought with us a high-SPF sunscreen. We really were.

We burrowed down into all the pillows and blankets and flipped slowly through the Ikea catalog together. I swear, if I had a tail I'd have been wagging it. "We're at Ikea, reading the Ikea catalog," Walter said, shaking his head, and I laughed. My mom teases us about the ways we haven't changed, and it's true. We've *always* liked to ogle a catalog together: Lego, Playmobil, Hammacher Schlemmer. Even something called Oriental Trading Company, although that one tends to depress us weirdly, with its twelve-packs of glow-in-the-dark plastic crucifixes and luau party supplies and inflatable cowboy hats. But there's nobody I'd rather be that kind of depressed with than Walter. In fact, maybe there's nobody besides Walter who would even *understand* that kind of depressed.

Do you know how you can just feel completely *strange* in the world sometimes? Like everyone's one way and you're another? Or like there's some translator chip that someone forgot to program you with, and other kids joke about stuff and you don't know what they're talking about? Or the teacher says something random—like maybe in science she's talking about genetics, about an experiment with "smooth and wrinkled peas"—and you suddenly hear your own laughter, the only sound of laughter in the room, coming from your own freakily laughing face? (Walter calls that particular thing *the laughing-out-your-laugh-hole problem*.) My parents once assured me that grown-ups feel that way too. "Thanks, guys," I said, teasing. "It's very reassuring to know that this is a permanent condition, rather than a phase I'm going through." But the thing is? I never feel strange with Walter. I mean, never when we're hanging out, just the two of us, obviously. But also never if he's even just in the room with me. He's like my own personal normalizer, and if he's in my class at school or at a party with me, or in a group of people, I can relax and just feel all right in the world.

"You're Frankie's knight in shining armor," my dad once said to Walter. He'd shown up at my swim meet on a Friday afternoon, and even though I'd swum terribly and was, in fact, a terrible swimmer, I yelled happily when I saw him. Walter had nodded at my dad. "I know," he'd said seriously. "She's mine too."

"KOPPAR table lamp," Walter was saying now.

"Same," I said, even though I'd closed my eyes for a second, just to rest them.

"TVINGEN hand towel," Walter said.

And I said . . . well, I don't actually know what I said next.

"Frankie, Frankie." Walter was shaking my shoulder.

"Frankie, wake up! We fell asleep." I saw the glowing numbers of Walter's watch in the dark: 8:58. The lights were out in our loft, and there was a roaring sound. When I peeked out, I could see a guy with a cap on and earphones, and a vacuum cleaner strapped onto him like a backpack. He was moving slowly through the showroom with his nozzle, passing it over the couches and carpets. When he reached the far wall, he turned off the machine, and the sudden quiet almost spooked me.

I felt like I could *smell* the vacuum cleaner—a metallic thickness, like the kind that's in the air before a thunderstorm.

Walter put a warning finger to his lips, took out his notebook and pen, scribbled something, and showed it to me. *How will we know when he's done?* he'd written, just as, with such perfect timing I almost laughed out loud, we heard the scratchily unmistakable sound of a switched-on walkie-talkie, heard the vacuum guy say, "Final clean. Nine o'clock checkout. Building all clear."

And I wrote back, *That's how.*

11

Couches and Color Schemes

My dad likes to tell this story about the first time they took Walter and me to see fireworks—how we were so excited we couldn't stop talking. My dad does a really funny imitation of our squeaky little preschool voices: "Is it going to be such a big, big *spway* of *lights* acwoss the whole entire *sky*?" "It's going to make such a loud, loud sound! A loud, loud *noise*, even!" On and on. We couldn't shut up, apparently, and we had our little Fourth of July glow bracelets on and we were singing "The Star-Spangled Banner" and squealing, we were so excited, sitting together on our blanket under the deepening blue. And then finally it was dark, and the first fireworks spangled the sky with a huge splintering boom. When Walter and I didn't say anything, the parents looked over and saw that we'd fallen asleep, leaning against each other with our thumbs in our mouths.

I guess we hadn't changed that much. We'd started our big Ikea adventure by *falling asleep*.

But we were awake now, and we were loose in Ikea. Because we'd lost an hour, we rushed at first, grabbing our backpacks and creeping down the ladder, crouching behind a fuzzy blue couch at the bottom, like spies. As far as we could tell, lights were on in some places, and other parts of the store looked dark. The vacuum-cleaner smell had evaporated, and now the store smelled like it did in the daytime: cinnamon-y and new and very, very clean. It was super quiet. My voice, when I used it, sounded loud in my ears: "Cool" was all I said, and Walter whispered back, "Cool. And creepy." "Showroom tour?" I asked, whispering now, and Walter whispered back, "Showroom tour."

The first thing we wanted to do was—don't laugh—just, kind of, sit in all the showrooms. Most of them are like a single room in a house—a kitchen, a bathroom, a living room. But our favorites are the ones that are like a whole miniature apartment—yes, a tiny house—with a little kitchen and table and living area and sleeping loft, all right there in a space as big as a single room. We crept into one now, breathless and half expecting to see someone. But after a few minutes on the couch, we relaxed a little bit, pretended we lived there. "This is my dream color scheme," Walter was saying. "Everything white and black and gray, with the little purple details—the cushions and the blankets. If this were our house, I'd be so glad we'd decided to decorate this way."

There was one of those classic lotus-shaped light fixtures above us—the kind that looks like a big white plastic flower. They are one of my very favorite things about Ikea. "You could get a light fixture like that, if you wanted," my mom said once. "They're not even that expensive. Ask Grandma for your birthday." But the thing is? I don't want it in our kind of shabby house with all its old, mismatched stuff. I want the light fixture *here*, where it looks perfect with everything else.

Walter and I stood up and wandered into a different pretend apartment. "This is my exact *not* color scheme," Walter said in a loud whisper. "Barf green. Depressing fake plants everywhere. A cowhide or fake-cowhide rug. A horse-racing poster." He sat down on a black leather couch.

"I hate leather furniture," he said. And I said, "That's because you're a vegetarian and you're morally opposed to leather."

"And because it's *nasty*," he said. "It's very manly, though," he added. "I mean, you've got to give it that."

We sat quietly for a minute. "You're going to be surprised to hear me say this," Walter finally said. "But I might be kind of *done* sitting in the showrooms, at least for now."

"Good timing," I said, "because I am too. Where do you most want to go next?"

"Bedding department," Walter said. "I want to pile up all the comforters, like, *tons* of them, and jump on them and hide under them."

"Epic blanket fort," I said. "A mature and important plan. Come on, then. It isn't exactly going to build itself."

We looked both ways, darting through the deserted showroom from couch to couch. When we rounded the corner into the area with all the bed displays, it was dark. Not pitch-black dark, because light was still filtering in from other parts of the store, but kind of twilight-dim. "Perfect!" Walter said. "This is just how I pictured it. It's cozier this way."

We decided that what we really had to do first was lie in every single bed, so we kicked off our shoes, dumped our packs, and started making the rounds. The beds were all so incredibly inviting, with loads of pillows, all stacked and arranged just so. "How come my bed at home always looks like the kind from a prison cell or like a cot from the Madeline books?" I asked Walter, lying back on a particularly cushiony bed that was covered in a gray polka-dotted comforter.

"'In an old house in Paris that was covered with vines lived twelve little girls in two straight lines,'" Walter said dreamily, quoting *Madeline*.

"Yes, okay, but seriously. I try to prop the pillows up all ploofy and nice, but it always looks so flat or something."

"Maybe because you actually sleep on it?" Walter offered. "Or because it's an actual real bed and you only have two pillows instead of"—he craned around to count them all, including the little decorative ones—"um, eleven?"

"Maybe," I said, and sighed. We hoisted ourselves

up and plopped down on another bed. Another awesomely comfortable bed.

"It's like 'Goldilocks and the Three Bears,'" Walter said, stretching. "*Ahhh. This bed's juuuust right.* Only we feel like that about every single bed."

"Remember when we were little," I said, "and you told me you wanted a water bed?"

Walter laughed. "Yes. *I would never put sheets on it, though! Then how would I see all the pretty fish?*"

Walter had somehow imagined that a water bed was going to be a kind of aquarium, but one that you got to sleep on. So then I imagined it that way too, only after that we went to a birthday party where we'd heard that the parents actually had a water bed. "Excuse me, but where is all your pretty, pretty fish?" Walter had asked politely, after we'd snuck into their bedroom to peel back the sheets. "And why is your water bed not see-through?" The parents explained why, and they were actually really nice about it, but we were very, *very* disappointed.

Now we lay on flowered beds and swirled ones, on paisley and striped beds, dark beds and pale, and on each one I lay back and closed my eyes and imagined how my life would be if that were my bed. I mean,

I'd still be me, of course. The girl who all the town librarians knew by name. The one who liked algebra and looking at online restaurant menus and at the huge album of Mr. Pockets's baby pictures. The one her fifth-grade teacher described as "A very diligent student. Responsible, well behaved, and conscientious. Generally well liked, but with limited substantial peer friendships." This was on a report I found on my father's bedside table. "Oh, Frankie, honey, don't read that," my mom had said, finding me reading it. "I think that some of your teachers stress out about you not being part of, like, a big group of girls talking about lip gloss or French braids or whatever. It's so stupid. I know you know that."

I did know that. But if I had this bed, all these pillows, everything so clean and nice, then . . . what? I think I'd feel like I was floating. Like everything was just right, all the time. Even though it would only be a bed.

"Can you be, like, a professional bed tester?" Walter asked. "As a career?"

"I know!" I said. "I was just wondering that. Actually, I was wondering something kind of different, which is whether you could just be an Ikea design consultant, where they'd call you in to look at stuff, and you'd say if you liked it or not. That would be my dream job, I think."

"You'd be terrible at it, no offense," Walter said. "You like everything."

This was kind of true. I couldn't even put my finger on why I liked everything so much. It had something to do with the fact that none of my stuff was here—even though I liked my stuff, right? Or I wouldn't have it. Would I? All my collections. All the stuff I wanted, but then actually having it made everything feel so cluttery and tiring.

When Walter and I were six or seven, my parents took us to a geology exhibit at a museum a couple towns over, and we stopped at the souvenir shop afterward. For three dollars, you could fill a little velvet drawstring bag with colorful polished stones from a huge barrel, and Walter and I both decided to do it, digging the money out from our coin purses and paying for the bags before spending thirty or forty minutes filling and refilling them with different collections of shiny pink and green and blue rocks. It was so much fun. Only once we'd settled on our choices, we got back in the car and sat quietly with our rock bags for a few minutes before Walter said, "I guess I really just wanted to *pick out* the rocks. Because now that I have them? I don't actually want them that much." I felt the exact same way. Sometimes I think that's kind of what stuff is like. You want it until you have it, and then it's like the light inside it goes out.

"'Memory foam'?" Walter was saying, reading the tag on a pillow. "Do people have a lot of memories about foam? Does foam have memories of its own?"

"Deep," I said.

Walter started stripping the beds, piling pillows and comforters on the floor. I grabbed big armfuls and added them to the pile until it was a shoulder-high heap of colorful, patterned softness. Walter was bouncing up and down on one of the beds, and he suddenly leapt high into the air and landed with a cushiony thud on the bedding mountain. I scrambled up onto the bed and sproinged into the pile after him. We took turns. We jumped at the same time and landed together in a muffled, laughing heap. We lay on our backs, slowly sinking as the air escaped, the pile deflating beneath us while we got swallowed up in pillows and quilts, like quicksand, but made of cotton and feathers.

"Do you remember when my dad used to tell us the 'Princess and the Pea' story?" Walter asked now.

Of course I did. Walter's dad was the most incredible storyteller, and he could tell you a story you knew inside out—"Rumpelstiltskin," say, or "Rapunzel"—in such an exciting way that you'd be on the edge of your seat wondering what would happen next, even though if you stopped to think about it, of course you actually already *knew* that the straw would get spun into gold or that the princess would tumble her braid out the window and be rescued.

"That was always one of my favorites," I said. "*Eighteen, nineteen, twenty feather beds!*" I spoke in Walter's dad's deep storytelling voice. "I think it's kind of funny. I mean, I know they're trying to prove she's a real princess or whatever. But it always seems like the kind of person who wouldn't be able to sleep because of a pea under her twenty feather beds would actually be super annoying to live with. *I couldn't sleep a wink because I could hear an ant walking around in the toolshed!*" I laughed at my own example. "Also, confusingly,

I always pictured, like, a soft green pea, instead of a hard dried pea, which made the whole story that much more strange and amazing."

Walter was quiet. I'd been staring up at the ceiling—or at the industrial tangle of pipes way up where a normal ceiling would be—but now I flipped over onto one elbow to look at my friend. His eyes were closed. "Oh, Walter," I said, and shook my head. I draped my arm over him and squeezed his shoulder. "Walter."

12

The Thing We Weren't Talking About

You're going to hate this, that I left this part of the story out until now. But the thing is? Walter's dad is dead. He died at the end of last year, from brain cancer. It was quick and it was terrible, and Walter and his mom and Zeke were sad beyond sad. Were and are still. I know it's nothing like how bad it is for them, but the truth is that my family has been really sad too. Walter's dad was my dad's best friend, for one thing. And for another, he was just the greatest. Funny, fun, interesting, and even, if this isn't too weird to say, crazily handsome. I once overheard my mom, in tears, saying to my dad, "Don't you always feel like it's the nicest and best people who die young? I mean, you're never like, *Oh well, too bad, but at least that guy was kind of a jerk.*" Only she said something worse than *jerk*. When she saw me standing there, she said, "Oh, honey, sorry." And I said, "That's okay. I understand." Which was true.

"Do you remember the last time he told us a story?" Walter asked now, his voice thick, and I did. Of course I did. Walter's dad had been propped up on their couch under a heap of blankets, with a mug of tea balanced in his lap—a mug that said, *If at first you don't succeed, skydiving isn't for you.* "I'm sorry, Frankie, but I'm feeling too low today to use the sad mug you gave me," he'd said. It was, in fact, an especially tragic specimen from my collection, with lumpy hearts that the potter had stuck on and glazed a speckled brown. "But you know I love it."

It was the last week of his life, although we didn't understand that yet, and I was over at their house because I was always over at their house. "You should tell Frankie that you guys need just-family time," I once heard my mom say over the phone to Walter's mom, but she told me after that Alice had said, "Frankie *is*

86

family. And Walter could use her company, if it doesn't make her uncomfortable to be here." It did make me a little uncomfortable, to tell you the truth, but I gathered up my courage because I wanted to be there.

Anyway, we were sitting on the floor, leaning against the couch, and Walter's dad was pretty weak by then, kind of confused because of the pressure the tumor was putting on his brain, but he was telling us the story of Cinderella. I'm sure it sounds babyish, but it wasn't. He was so good at exaggerating all the dark and peculiar parts of fairy tales—all the cruelty and terror and magic—so that you never felt like you were just skipping along boringly toward a happy ending. As he told it, the story always involved Cinderella rescuing herself. She doesn't even end up marrying the prince in his version—they just become really close friends.

"And there was a great and terrible glittering," Walter's dad was saying. "Like a thousand jagged shards on the palace steps. And the prince bent down and, lo and behold, it was not a brokenness there on the steps at all. It was the princess's glass—"

Walter's dad shook his head, the way you would if there were a fly buzzing in your face. He gave us a puzzled expression. He wrinkled his nose and squinted.

"Shipwreck?" he said, and shook his head again. "Wait, wait. Don't tell me. The princess's glass . . . *shipwreck*?" he said again, and laughed. "I know it's not that. That's, like, the *Titanic*. Ack, sorry, guys. This is odd. I see the other word, right behind that word, but I can't seem to say it."

"*Slipper,*" Walter said, smiling, and his dad slapped his own forehead.

"Duh!" he said. "Of course. *Shipwreck*." And then he laughed and we laughed. Then he sighed and said *shipwreck* once more before saying, "I think I'm just going to say *shoe*."

That was not the last time I got to see Walter's dad, but it was the last *good* time. After that, it was a lot of sleeping and drifting away. A little bit of muttering and not much actual talking. He was taking a lot of painkillers by then, and they made him even more dozy and out of it than he'd already been. He woke up once and said, "It's like a *phantom* phantom limb. Everyone thinks it's gone, but it's actually still there!" before falling back asleep.

I wasn't there when he actually died, but Walter said it was weirdly peaceful. Walter and his mom and

Zeke lay in bed with him. "And he just kind of *went somewhere else*. It's hard to explain." Walter had tried to explain it to me anyway. "I don't know if I really believe in heaven or anything like that?" he'd said, wiping his nose on his sleeve. "But I did feel like he was more *going away* than disappearing. So I guess I'm not sure what I think anymore. But don't tell me that he lives on in my heart, Frankie. That's what my mom's aunt Ellen told me, and it was really kind of annoying."

"I would never," I said.

Walter squeezed my wrist and said, "Sorry. I know you wouldn't."

At the funeral, my dad spoke and told the story about a trip we'd all taken together to Maine, and how Walter's dad had said from his beach towel, as the sun was setting, "Everything I need is right here. Ocean, sand, air, friends, wife, kids, lobster rolls, saltwater taffy, clouds." He was the kind of person who really liked to be happy, and was.

Afterward, Walter had played "The Long and Winding Road" on the piano and everybody cried. Zeke lay awkwardly in Alice's lap like a bag of arms and legs, then he leaned up and over the back of the pew to whisper to me and my parents the thing he'd heard everyone saying to his own family: "I'm so sorry for your loss."

"Thank you, Zeke, honey," my mom had whispered back, crying. "I'm so sorry for yours too."

13

Comforters and Feathers

Now, in the bedding fort, seeing Walter so sad made my ribs hurt. "Tell me," I said. I shook his shoulder a little, like I could rattle his feelings out of him. "Talk to me." But he only shook his head, swallowed like he could swallow the feelings away. So I did the only thing I could think of: I picked up a pillow and whacked him on the head. A slow smile spread across his face and he sat up. "Oh no you didn't!" he said, and he picked up an even bigger pillow and swung it around so that it thudded into me. We ended up throwing pillows and whipping them around, hitting each other and ducking and laughing so hard that I had to squat down at some point to catch my breath.

"Oh god, are you peeing in your pants again?" Walter said, laughing, and I let him have it with a gigantic pillow. I pummeled him.

"That was, like, six years ago. And we were on a *Ferris wheel*. And I was terrified!"

"Just saying," Walter said, and he crashed my head between two pillows like they were cymbals.

We'd hit some pendant lamps above us, and they were swinging in crazy arcs, though they weren't turned on, at least. And of course, like in a cartoon, one of the pillows split open so that there were feathers everywhere, spraying up into the air and then drifting down.

"I feel like we're in a giant snow globe," Walter said, breathless, still hitting me methodically with a long body pillow that was like a giant white sausage. I fell backward onto what was left of our pillow mountain, panting, while the feathers floated past and stuck to our sweaty faces. Walter threw down the giant pillow, then leapt after it and landed with a *phloomp*.

We propped ourselves up on our elbows to check out the damage. There were pillows and comforters and feathers everywhere, like a giant bedding bomb had exploded nearby. Walter pointed to a sign, and we laughed. It said NO PILLOW FIGHTS.

"What now?" I said.

"If this were a kids' movie, we'd move on to the next scene and the cleanup would kind of just . . . happen." Walter looked around and pulled his mouth into a comical grimace.

"I know," I said. "I feel like kids do crazy things and learn important lessons, but the boring details of what happens next don't really make it into the stories." I could practically hear my mom saying, "If you don't clean it up, someone else is going to have to," which was kind of annoying.

But we cleaned up anyway, because we've always been *Such. Good. Kids.* We dragged all the covers and pillows back to the beds where they belonged. We remade the beds, tucking in sheets and blankets, re-creating the inviting piles of pillows as well as we could, folding up the extra duvets and shaking the feathers off everything. It was definitely not the funnest part of our adventure so far. It was, in fact, kind of like cleaning up at home, only bigger.

There were still feathers everywhere, though, and

Ikea didn't sell anything helpful like a vacuum cleaner we could borrow. I pictured the guy we'd seen earlier, with the vacuum strapped to his back. There must have been cleaning supplies somewhere, but we didn't know where to look for them. We tried one door that led only to a demo closet, a row of perfect, bare hangers gleaming inside. Another door led to a demo pantry, with rows and rows of empty mason jars. Walter sighed. "Sheesh," he said. "There must be real stuff somewhere. But where?" We gave up. I tore a page out of my notebook and we wrote a note that said, simply, *We are so sorry about the mess!* We left it on top of the torn pillow. Then we picked up our packs and headed for the cafeteria. We were starving.

14

Free Refills

Not to be all foreshadow-y, but this was around the time I started to have the feeling that we were being followed. It was when we were creeping toward the cafeteria. I'd hear footsteps behind us, or I'd think I did, but then I'd turn around and they'd stop. Or I'd see a shadow flicker across the wall, but it would disappear when I looked right at it. I didn't say anything to Walter. There is nothing worse than someone contaminating you with their crazy worries when you're just trying to have a good time. Or when you're trying not to be too worried yourself.

The cafeteria was amazing enough to distract me,

though. I've thought a lot about the expression *like a kid in a candy store*. For one thing, when I was little, I imagined that exact thing all the time: going to a candy store and getting to have anything and everything I wanted. Marzipan fruits and all the different soda flavors of jelly beans and the maple-sugar maple leaves and sour gummy grapefruit slices. "What about chocolate?" Walter used to say, in a whisper, because we talked about it when we were supposed to be napping in kindergarten, and I'd shrug and whisper, "Nah. What about you?" And Walter would say, "Chocolate. Just chocolate. And also chocolate with marshmallows in it." And then Mrs. Hawk would shush us and we'd put our heads back down on our nap blankets. "Also chocolate with *coconut*," Walter would whisper. "And caramel. With chocolate."

But also, about that expression—*kid in a candy store*? The idea that you could have anything you wanted has always been very appealing to me. I guess that's a dumb thing to say. I mean, who doesn't it appeal to? It's like how when I was six I confessed to my parents that I wished I could see more people naked, and my dad said, "Oh, Frankie, honey, *everybody* wishes they could see more people naked." It turns out that people all kind of want the same things.

Now Walter and I really *were* like kids in a candy store, even though there wasn't actually much candy there.

The hot stuff had been put away, but we filled glasses with sour red lingonberry soda from the bright metal drink machine and helped ourselves to plastic-wrapped plates of Swedish cake: apple cake and almond cake, pink-iced slices of sponge cake and dark wedges of chocolate torte, little green logs of something and little coconut-covered balls of something else. Walter already had three plates of chocolate torte in one hand, a glass of soda in the other.

I must have hesitated because Walter said, "What?"

"I don't know," I said. "If we take all this stuff, then we'll be stealing. I hadn't thought about that before."

Walter nodded. "I hadn't thought of that either." He sighed. "I love how we're willing to trick our parents and trespass and, hello, *spend the night in Ikea*—but not to take cake. But I get it. It's wrong. I feel the same way."

"We could leave money," I said, and Walter nodded. "Let's."

Altogether it seemed like it would add up to six dollars and change, so I counted out the money from the little pocket of my pack and left it near a cash register, shrugging. "Yay for dork criminals!" Walter said, and high-fived me.

"Speaking of dorks," I said, "can we go eat in one of the kitchen showrooms? I've always wanted to eat at one of those nice high kitchen islands with the stools." Walter flashed me a classic Walter smile and stuck his two thumbs in the air, and we crept out of the cafeteria.

Walter followed me—which at least explained, for that moment, the being-followed feeling—to the exact kitchen I'd always loved: everything sleek and black and white, with sleek black stools pulled up to a sleek white counter. We set out our plates and cups, and Walter went around to the other side of the island. "How's the cake, guys?" he asked in a pretty decent imitation of my mom. "Can you taste the food coloring in the pink frosting? I worry that you can actually taste it. Tell me if you can. Is it dry? I might have over-baked it."

"Dooon't," I groaned. "I am seriously not here so

that we can act out scenes from my life with the recipe developer."

"Okay," Walter said, laughing. "But you do know how lucky you are, right? I mean, your mom's always like, 'Walter, honey, I'm so sorry, but would you mind tasting this caramel popcorn I'm trying to figure out? And washing it down with this caramel milk shake?' And, um, no, I don't mind, actually! Plus, even regular dinner is good at your house."

This was definitely true, and I felt bad suddenly, because Walter's dad used to be the person who cooked dinner in their family, and his mom was stuck taking over. "Who likes mac and cheese?" she always said, half joking, half apologizing, and Zeke would say, totally serious, "I do, Mom! It's my favorite!"

"Don't feel bad," Walter said, because of being a mind reader (at least of me). "I didn't mean it like that. Just that I love eating at your house."

"I know," I said. "I'm glad."

While we sat, eating our cake, Walter figured out that spinning on the stools actually made them go up and down on some kind of giant screw. We spun and spun, racing our stools to the bottom and then back up to the top, until we were dizzy and laughing and cake crumbs were spraying everywhere. "I like the view from down here!" Walter kept announcing, before spinning his stool up like crazy and saying, "But I prefer it up here!" He was in his classic deranged-Walter mood, and for me it was like gulping air again after being underwater for too long.

I ate my cake for a while, admiring the wall behind the stove. It was made of the prettiest blue-green glass tiles, which looked a little like sea glass, but not as frosty. Walter looked where I was looking. "I don't even understand the point of the backwash," he said. I laughed.

"Back*splash*," I said. "That's the fancy wall behind a stove. Back*wash* is when you take a sip of someone's soda and some of it goes back into the can from your mouth."

"Dude," Walter said. "Yuck."

The shelves above the stove were lined with canning jars full of dried beans and pasta and nuts—only when you looked closely, you could see that they were just photos of beans and pasta and nuts that had been stuck in the jars and kind of bent around. I thought about my kitchen at home—the canning jars filled with my mom's actual good salsa and plum jam and bread-and-butter pickles.

But I didn't have time to get overly philosophical just then. Walter looked at his watch and grabbed my hand. "Oh man," he said. "It's almost midnight. What next, Frankinella?"

15

What Next?

What next was a doorknob. I had this idea, still, that I
could get one here, and it would improve my life. I said
this to Walter, and he said, "You should write a self-help
book. *Get a Doorknob, Improve Your Life!*" I laughed. It
really didn't sound like such an inspired program for
happiness. But I'd be lying if I told you that the massive display of drawer knobs and handles filled me with
anything other than joy and longing. Row after row
of perfect knobs, all organized like a grid on a wall of
sparkling clear plastic. The knobs were brass and shiny
steel; they were glass and ceramic and plastic in rainbow colors. You could pull the tester knob so that a

little transparent drawer opened, and what was in the drawer was more of that same kind of knob. Ridiculous perfection.

"Man," I sighed. "I forgot how much I love this place."

Walter laughed. "Um, Frankie? No you didn't."

I was touching a smooth turquoise knob, spacing out.

"Uh-oh!" Walter said. "Did a case of the wanties come to Frankietown?"

The wanties is what we call that sudden feeling you get when you *have to* have something. We get it all the time when we're playing the picking game. I mean, in the craziest way. Walter and I can even get the wanties from this catalog called Petrossian that is, I'm not kidding, just a bunch of different kinds of smoked fish, which Walter doesn't even eat, and also caviar, which neither of us has ever even tasted. The wanties come, and then you have to try to let them go. Once when I talked to my mom about spending some of my birthday money to order something from a toy catalog—I think it was a plastic gun that shot out plastic sushi, maybe—she said, "How about you sleep on it, Frankie? If you're still thinking about it tomorrow, we'll order it then." Sure enough, I forgot all about it as soon as the catalog was put away.

That's what I was thinking about now, touching a display knob. How rare it was to feel actually satisfied by things, however nice they were. I didn't really need a turquoise knob, however much I felt like I wanted it. What I probably needed to do was talk to my parents about the door situation, even though it made me squirm to imagine the conversation. And, like a metaphor for my nervousness, a shadow flitted into my peripheral vision. I whipped my head around to look, but there was nothing there.

"What?" Walter said, nervous.

And I said, "Nothing. I'm being plagued by my own conscience." I laughed unconvincingly.

"Did you see something, Frankie?"

"No. I totally don't think I did," I said. And Walter pulled his eyebrows together just as we heard a rustling, or a maybe-rustling, like when you're lying in bed, listening to a sound in the walls—mice, probably—but your cat is standing dead still on the dresser, with his ears pointed straight up, freaking you out a little bit.

Out of nowhere, an alarm sounded right by us, and Walter grabbed my arm and yanked me into a bedroom showroom, pointed to a sign that said ROOM FOR UNDERBED STORAGE!, and dragged me beneath the bed frame.

It was pitch-black. Walter's voice floated into my face from an inch away, the sound of him whispering "Underbed storage," which made me laugh. "You think underbed storage is funny?" he whispered, and then I couldn't stop laughing, in that terrible way where you're trying to be quiet so you're laughing silently, but then suddenly you have to take a big, gasping breath.

"Frankie!" Walter shushed me, and I tried to quiet down so we could listen, but I couldn't hear anything. "Do you think this is real wood or veneer?" Walter whispered, which was not particularly funny, but I started laughing again anyway.

After a few minutes Walter whispered, "Oh my gosh, you are going to kill me."

"What?" I said.

"That sound? I think I accidentally set the kitchen timer on the stove we were looking at. I think that ringing was just the timer going off."

A perfectly logical explanation! And yet, if there were a nervousness scale that went up to ten, I'd say we were at about a five at this point. You know, or a seven.

As we climbed out from under the bed, Walter put a hand to his chest and said, "Heart! Still! Pounding!" but then became immediately distracted by a gigantic piece of furniture. He read the tag. "Oooh," he said. "It's a *wardrobe*! A wardrobe seems like such a cool thing. But maybe I'm just thinking of the Narnia books. *The Lion, the Witch, and the Closet* just doesn't have the same ring to it."

Next to the wardrobe was a floor lamp that looked like a frilly nightie on a stand. It was the creepiest thing I'd ever seen at Ikea. "I hope you like it," Walter said, and smiled. "I already got it for you for your birthday."

"It's perfect," I said. "It's like my grandma, but in lamp form."

The room was set up as a display of how grown-ups and children could share a single room in a small apartment: the kids' sleeping area was sectioned off with a long white curtain, and there were pretty strings of flags draped around it. I loved it. The truth is that I'd slept in my parents' room until I was way too old to. They kept a mattress on the floor for me, and more nights than not I ended up there. I stopped eventually because it just felt too babyish unless I was sick, but sometimes I wished I still could. Or that I still *felt* like

I could, I guess, since technically I could have. Are you wanting to remind me that I'm the same person complaining about the lack of privacy at my house? I know. I don't understand it either.

"Ugh," Walter said. Apparently he did not feel the same way as me about the cute rooming option.

"What?"

"I don't know." He shrugged, looked away. "My mom makes Zeke and me sleep in her room now. You know, since my dad died." He wrinkled up his nose and touched a blue flag on the curtain.

"What do you mean she *makes* you?" I said. I couldn't exactly picture Alice making Walter do anything.

"She doesn't *make* us make us. But she's always like, 'Come cuddle with me,' and then she falls asleep. Sometimes I try to wriggle out from under her arm, but then she wakes up and says something like, 'Oh, am I driving you crazy? I am, aren't I?' And then I feel terrible. I don't want to hurt her feelings. I know she's lonely or freaked out or whatever."

"Oh," I said.

I knew Walter had been . . . I guess the word is *depressed*, since his dad died. But I had wanted to imagine that he was feeling better all the time, as if grief were a rocket zooming away in one direction, getting smaller and smaller as time passed. I was starting to understand that it wasn't like that. Partly because Walter was getting more Walter-y at Ikea, and it made me realize how much I'd missed him. And partly because here, outside of our real lives, inside this pretend world, he was starting to seem less like a too-full glass that you have to carry really carefully so that you don't spill it. Maybe because everything was starting to spill, so we could finally just relax now. I'm not sure.

"That sucks," I said, and took an uncertain step toward him. Maybe he wanted to talk more?

But whatever Walter was wanting to say, he'd already said it. Now he was touching a mirror. "FRÄCK mirror," he said. "That's kind of an awkward name in English. 'Ugh, I dropped the frack mirror!' 'This fracking mirror!'" He put an arm around my shoulders and we leaned in to look at ourselves. A REFLECTION OF GOOD VALUE! the sign said. I touched the glass where a tear sparkled in Walter's reflection—then I turned and wiped it from his actual cheek. "Feelings," he said, and laughed, shook his head. "Ugh." Then he turned away.

16

Things Tilt

Walter grabbed my hand again and dragged me, running, from room to room until we got to the couches. Oh, we loved the couches. We sat on wine-colored velvet couches and scratchy gray tweed ones, on smooth cotton couches in Easter-egg colors and shiny, slippery ones that Walter slid off, over and over, on-purpose-by-accident, saying "Whoops!" every time, like he was in a bad old comedy film.

If I were going to pick a single moment when our night started to shift, I might pick this one. Mostly what we'd thought we'd wanted to do at Ikea was enjoy the furniture, spend time with all the nice stuff. It wasn't like we had a big list of wacky ideas. When we were little, we'd loved to play house. This was a lot like that. Only, you know, overnight in a giant empty store, illegally.

We never imagined that this activity—the activity of simply being there—would grow dull. And it didn't, exactly. Or maybe it did. Because instead of sitting around quietly for the rest of the night, we started to get ourselves in trouble.

We were squashed into a pink love seat, and Walter was tapping his foot restlessly. He tipped his head back and pointed up. The way they're displayed in the showroom, there are, like, a hundred couches on the floor, but then, to save space, there are, like, a hundred more attached to the wall, one on top of another, like shelves made of couches. Walter was pointing to a huge soft-looking brown one that was suspended about three feet below where the metal beams and ducts started, up near the ceiling. "Want to maybe sit up there?" he asked. "I'll bet the view is great." I shook my head.

I am not unafraid of heights.

"Hello?" I said. "Remember me? Your friend Frankie, the only kid in fifth grade who couldn't do the high ropes course because she couldn't *get up to* the high ropes course?" This was a field trip we'd taken to one of those terrifying outdoor adventure places, where you have to challenge yourself to climb and dangle from various treacherous balancing and trapeze situations strung between the trees. Let me just say: I'd done really well at what the instructors called the "low elements."

Walter smiled. "You almost got up to it! You were amazing, and you know it."

That made me laugh. I was *not* amazing, and I did know it. Although, after the ropes course fiasco, when I was feeling pretty low (no pun intended) on the bus back to school, Walter had split his granola bar, handed me half, and said, "Climbing those three rungs scared took way more courage than climbing to the top *not* scared."

"You're a very encouraging person," I had said back, and then thought about the word *courage* inside the word *encourage*. When you encourage somebody, maybe what you do is try to put a little of your own courage inside them. It's amazing how well it can work.

"Go for it," I said. "I am totally here for you."

Walter shrugged, leapt up, and started scrambling up the couches like they were rock-climbing ledges, sitting in each one briefly before climbing to a higher one. I walked over to stand below, offering up dumb nervous advice, like, "Be careful!"

"Wait," Walter yelled down. "What? *Do* or *don't* be careful?"

"Ha-ha," I said. Then said again, annoyingly, "Seriously, Walter. Be careful."

Walter stood and reached up to the highest couch, was stretching and leaning back to pull himself up to it, when a ringing started again, right near us. Walter lost his balance and grabbed at a brown cushion, which came away from the couch, so that he fell holding the cushion on top of him, like the world's most useless safety apparatus. Like on an airplane, when you're supposed to use your seat cushion as a flotation device, only there was no water, and Walter was falling backfirst, the cushion clutched to his chest. "Falling!" he said, redundantly, as he fell, bouncing off one wider couch and then grazing the others while I stood with my hand over my mouth in terror. Walter landed with a gentle thud on the carpet next to me and said, "Oof," then rose and shook himself off like a dog.

"Oh my god," I said. "Walter. Are you okay?" And he was. I could see that he was.

The ringing started up again—or kept going. I wasn't sure which.

"Kitchen timer?" I said, and Walter shook his head, pointed to a phone on the wall—an old-looking phone, with a cord and everything—that was still ringing.

"Should we get that, do you think?"

"No," I said. I couldn't tell if he was serious or not.

But he hopped over, lifted the receiver, and said jauntily, "Hello, Ikea couch department!" He looked puzzled for a second, then said "Hello?" again, shrugged, and put the phone back in its cradle. "I thought I heard someone breathing," he said. "But then there was a click. Wrong number, probably. Maybe we shouldn't answer if it rings again."

I didn't say, "Maybe we shouldn't have answered it the first time either," but the words were in my mouth.

And then I remembered this weird thing that happened for a while after Walter's dad died. The phone would ring, and Zeke would say, "Maybe it's Dad, right? I just mean *maybe*." His eyebrows would be raised, the corners of his mouth turning up in a smile. Honestly, you just felt so bad for him. "No, honey," Walter or his mom would say, scooping him into a cuddle. Or, "I don't think so, Zekey-Deke." But Walter confessed to me that he had the same feeling. The phone would ring, and he'd feel a kind of vague hopefulness somehow. Ringing phones can be like that. Or, in this case, the opposite of that, I guess.

Walter pointed to the brown couch and took my hand. "Come," he said. "Let's do this."

And we did.

Or, I should say, we *sort of* did. Walter coached me up, couch to couch, offering me a hand from above, then scrambling down to boost me from below. "Gather up your courage," he said to me, which is what he'd said when I was two rungs up at the ropes course. "Gather it up and use it like a muscle." I was scared, and then more scared, and then—surprisingly—*less* scared. It was actually higher than I thought, but I could feel the strength in my arms as I stretched up to grab each couch, and I felt safe because of, well, Walter. When we got to the top, Walter lurched up onto the seat of the couch, then turned around to grab me under my armpits, which made me scream and laugh it tickled so much. I almost fell, but didn't. "Frankie. Frankie, my friend. Get ahold of yourself," Walter said, laughing, and he hauled me up the rest of the way. We sat back, panting. We were just sitting there, relaxing, but, you know, way up in the air. We could see out over the tops of all the fake walls, across the whole entire floor.

"This is the life," I said. And then, a minute later, "Is this the life or what?"

"This is the life," Walter agreed. Then he kicked his legs a little, and the couch rocked.

"Don't," I said but he was kicking more, and the couch—which seemed to be attached with some kind of metal cable—swung out a little bit from the wall. "Oh my god, Walter, I'm serious. Don't!" I said.

"Sorry," he said mischievously, pumping his legs now like we were on a swing.

"I am officially killing you," I said, but we heard the tearing even as my words were still hanging in the air, even as *we* were still hanging in the air, because the couch had torn away from the wall and dropped onto the couch below. Walter and I hung suspended for a second, like Wile E. Coyote over a cliff, before we dropped down on top of the cushions with a *thwoomp*. And then the weight was too much, and that second couch tore away and dropped, and the one below it, and the one below that—Walter and me bouncing along, bump, bump, bump, crash, crash, until we landed on a teetering tower of couches five couches high.

Someone was screaming—it was me, actually, I realized—and also laughing—this was also me—and we were perched still on our same brown couch, on top of all the other couches, with plaster dust from the wall in a cloud around our heads. I was laughing and laughing now, and Walter was too, and I said, "Oh my god, Walter," just at the moment that the tower of couches leaned one way—"Woooooah!"—and then the other—"Wooooah!"—and then undramatically kind of stabilized itself. Which was when the phone rang again.

17

Hide-and-Seek

We didn't answer the phone this time, although Walter jumped from the couch tower and darted over to it just as it stopped ringing. I had a bad feeling about that phone. Why would it be ringing in the night? It seemed like something from a scary movie—like you were going to answer it, and it was going to be someone calling you from the closet, where they were crouched with an ax. Not that I thought anyone was going to hurt us. But I was definitely starting to feel scared.

Which made this maybe not the best time to play hide-and-seek. Which is what I agreed to do anyway. "But wait," I said to Walter. "What about this?" I swept my arm toward the mess of couches, the carpet bunched beneath them, the wall torn above, and he shrugged.

"I don't know, Frankie."

"I'm not leaving another note," I said, and Walter nodded. "But I feel bad," I said, and Walter smiled.

"Too bad to play?" he said. Then he put his hands over his eyes and started counting.

What could I do? I ran to hide.

Playing hide-and-seek when you're already scared is fun, but also, well, terrifying. I've always loved and hated playing it with Walter. He is really good at being super quiet—and then scaring me half to death—and that's true even in someone's completely unscary *house*! In the dimly lit home-office showroom, it was a whole new level of creepy. When it was my turn to count to twenty, I didn't even hear him scampering into a spot. I crept around, looking under computer desks and behind file cabinets, my heart pounding in my ears, until a desk chair suddenly spun toward me.

"Boo!" Walter yelled, making me jump a hundred feet into the air.

"You're not supposed to jump out, you crazyhead!" I said, panting and laughing, my hand on my chest.

"You're supposed to stay hidden! Hello? *Hide*-and-seek? If I find you, I win."

"Then you win!" Walter said, and he grinned annoyingly.

While Walter counted, I managed to get myself wedged inside a wooden filing cabinet. "Ready or not!" I heard Walter yelling. "I'm going to get you, Frankie!" I wished he would be quieter. I was freaking myself out—enough that I wanted to get back out, but then the drawer was stuck and I couldn't open it from the inside. "Walter!" I yell-whispered. "Walter! I'm stuck! Get me out of here!" My knees were pressed up under my chin. "Walter!" But I heard him walking in the wrong direction, heard him rustling some curtains, his faint, faraway voice saying, "Aha!" and then, "Nope."

I waited. I jiggled the drawer, called out again, waited some more. Only when I heard footsteps again, they were coming from the wrong direction. And they were heavy ones. *Grown-up* ones.

Then I saw a beam of light swing past the keyhole. "Hello?" a voice said. It was not Walter's voice. "Hello? Is somebody in there?" The drawer handle rattled. I felt like I was going to faint. Luckily, my head was already between my knees. Isn't that the position you were supposed to be in for fainting? If I'd had a paper bag, I would have been breathing into it. But quietly.

"Hello?" An eye appeared in the keyhole, then disappeared again. *What would happen to us?* I wondered. I suddenly couldn't remember if they took kids to jail or not. I mean, I didn't think they did, but did they? Not permanently, I knew. But is that where we would end up for the night? That would be, like, the total opposite of Ikea. Worse. Why did I hide in a *drawer* of all things? Why was I asking myself so many questions?

"Hello? Hello? Open up!"

The handle rattled one final time, and then the drawer flew open, with me in it, and a flashlight was shining right into my face.

Not a flashlight. A headlamp. Walter's headlamp. With Walter's crazy, laughing self beneath it.

"Oh my god!" he said. "Oh my god. I got you so bad. Frankie! You should have seen the look on your face!" He was bent over, laughing.

"As soon as I catch my breath," I said, panting, "I am never speaking to you again."

"I know," he said, making his voice sound serious. But he was twinkling at me like a sky full of stars.

18

The Fun Cure

Next up was desk-chair races down the long hallway to the bathroom. "Each competing team is made up of a driver, who pushes the chair, and a rider who sits in the chair. Team A is you driving and me riding. Team B is the opposite." Classic Walter. He'd grabbed a timer from the kitchen area. "The rider is in charge of running the timer. Okay, I'm riding first. Ready . . . go!" We pushed each other down and back, timing ourselves and laughing. As you might imagine, we both won and lost every race.

While we were catching our breath, I spotted a table with a big box of the famous Ikea pencils: little wooden stubs that we had loads of at home because I can't help keeping a bunch every time we come— though even I admit they're not really that useful to have around, unless you're pretending to play mini golf, which we haven't done in a while.

Walter's dad, who had been all kinds of weird things in his life, like a puppeteer and a welder and a tofu maker, always had great ideas when it came to crazy contests. Pretend mini golf was a favorite when Walter and I were little, and it involved a rubber ball, a hockey stick, and various obstacles that Walter's dad created for us out of toys and Tupperware and furniture and figurines. It drove Walter's mom crazy. She'd come in, and we'd be crashing around with the stick, slamming into the coffee table and the fireplace, bunching up the rug and knocking books off the shelves, and she'd shake her head at us. "Alice, my darling!" he'd say, and grab her around the waist, dip her low to the ground, and kiss her. Then he'd hand her the hockey stick and bow, and she'd laugh and take a turn.

Walter's dad reminisced about it when he was sick. "Remember?" he said, half-asleep on the couch while Walter and I lay stomach-down on the floor, taking turns adding rooms to the dream house we were drawing. He'd been talking about a lot of fun things that day. Maybe he was kind of flipping through his mental catalog of the games he'd played with us, the experiments we'd done: the Lego build-a-thons and snow forts, the Mentos explosions and the light fixture we once made out of gummy bears, which glowed in a cool way before melting all over the place into gluey brown puddles. "Remember?" he said again. "Remember when we used to play mini groff? *Groff.* Mini groff?"

"Golf, Dad," Walter said patiently. He looked up and smiled at his father. "*Groff*'s the park near our house. Groff Park. Although we did once play *golf* in Groff, if that helps!"

"It does," Walter's dad had said, and sighed. "It helps a lot."

"Okay," I said now, and grabbed a huge handful of pencils, counted them out. "Twenty for you, twenty for me. It's the reality show called, uh, *What Can You Make with the Pencils?* and each contestant has one minute and twenty pencils. Got it? Contestants ready?" Walter and I were kneeling on a swirly gray carpet, our pencils in our hands. "Go!"

Did I mention that Walter's mom is an engineer? She is. She even consulted on the gigantic waterslide at our local amusement park, which meant that we got to go for free for a whole summer. So, yeah, maybe it kind of runs in the family. Because in one minute, I had managed only to organize my pencils into a lopsided sunburst, while Walter had built a perfect little roofless log cabin. Next I spelled the word *HELLO* and still had five pencils left over, while Walter built something like a suspension bridge using every last pencil. He can be annoying like that.

"Hey," he said, looking down at his creation, then looking up and tapping his chin. He waggled his eyebrows in what I was coming to know as his crazy-idea-at-Ikea expression. "Hey. Do you think we could rig up some sort of a zip line here?"

"Um, not really," I said. "No."

"A zip line," Walter said again.

"No."

"In the warehouse, maybe?" Walter was saying, like I hadn't answered twice already. "Should we?"

"No," I said. "Definitely not."

"Right?" Walter said, excited, and I sighed, because what are you going to do?

How effective is it to say no to Walter when he is being fully Walter? Um, *not at all effective.* Plus, he was giving me the dimple treatment. "Come on, Franks," he said (dimple, dimple). "It'll be awesome."

"I'm sure!" I said. "Plus, heights again! My fave."

"It's interesting," Walter said, smiling, "how at first it was *you* that was trying to talk *me* into everything—only now it's the other way around!"

"Yes," I said. I couldn't help smiling back at him. "That is very interesting. Why do you think?" If I could bottle and sell a night at Ikea, I was thinking, I could call it "The Fun Cure." I'd be a gazillionaire.

"Wait," I said. "Did I end up agreeing to this? I don't think I did." I had suddenly found myself standing with Walter in the giant, echoing warehouse, looking up. "There," he said, pointing to a steel beam in a high corner. "That's one anchoring spot. Over to . . ." He scanned the ceiling, studying the network of beams and ducts. "There," he said, pointing to a matching beam on the other side of the room. Remember: this is the kid of an engineer, so he also said some things to himself like, "If we account for the arc . . ." and "the definite integral," while I pretend-yawned.

I'll spare you the false starts. Because it took us a

long time to figure out what to make the line out of. We walked around looking at everything, and we'd find a sturdy something—like a SÄVERN shower curtain support, say—but then it would be way too short. And Walter had calculated that we needed at least a hundred feet of line. We looked at an extension cord in the lighting department, but Walter concluded that we'd have to knot together twenty of them, "And then it's going to be morning already." We looked at a retractable clothesline, decided it was too flimsy. Walter shook his head, did a little math with a pencil stub.

"Hey," I said, stopping short. We were passing through the textiles department, and there was a shelf with rolls of fabric stacked up on it. It was printed with geometric designs and foxes, with little owls and pretty leaves, all the nice Ikea things. "What about fabric, if we twisted it?"

Walter rubbed some of the sturdy fabric between his fingers. "Nice," he said, nodding. "Yes." He unrolled some, tugged on it to test its strength. "Do you know how long one of these rolls is?"

I thought back to helping out on a Thanksgiving photo shoot that my mom had styled the food for—

pictured the art director unrolling a piece of acorn-printed fabric across the wall and saying, "If it's a whole bolt, it should be a hundred yards." I told Walter this and he fist-bumped me. "Perfect," he said.

We picked a full-looking roll that was printed with a kind of wood-grain pattern—maybe birch—and we dumped it into a shopping cart and wheeled it over to the warehouse.

Fast-forward through Walter and me twisting a very long piece of fabric for a very long time, and then—also for a very long time—trying to figure out how to attach it securely to the beams. The warehouse is basically a grid of gigantically tall metal shelving, the same as at other big stores like Costco or Home Depot. Walter had scrambled up toward the top of a shelf and was leaning out to knot the fabric around a metal beam. I was standing down on the nice solid ground, sometimes covering my eyes with my hands, and sometimes yelling, "Walter, please!" as in *Walter, please be careful and don't fall and kill yourself.* The fabric was surprisingly heavy and awkward, and I had to help feed it up to where Walter was standing.

Did you ever hear of Philippe Petit, the acrobat

who walked a tightrope between the twin towers of the World Trade Center? Walter and I read a picture book about him when we were little, and then we saw a movie about him too. I was surprised to hear how long it took them to rig up the wire, and how heavy it all was, even though of course it made sense. I was also surprised by the idea of it: that someone would do something so crazily dangerous, just because they really, really wanted to. With nobody forcing them, and nothing to gain but just the experience itself. Anyway, I was thinking of that now, feeling glad that we were in an Ikea warehouse rather than a thousand feet above street level. This was alarming enough as it was.

Walter and I, but mostly Walter, got the fabric rope knotted so that it stretched from a high beam about halfway up on one side of the room across the big open part in the middle to a lower beam on the other side. Picture a tightrope, but angled downward. Walter tried testing the strength of his knot and ended up on the ground with the unhitched fabric in his hands, saying "Oof," and "Not actually strong enough." Watching him swing out like that with the fabric reminded me of Mr. Pockets as a kitten: he used to leap up onto the curtains and then swing out the window and back in, making me fret so much about losing him that we had to get screens put in. ("I want to keep you for all nine of your lives," I used to whisper to him.) Walter dusted himself off and climbed back up to re-knot the line.

Luckily, Walter's dad had spent a few days a couple summers ago teaching Walter and me a lot of useful knots. He called it "Knot Camp," and Walter's mom would come home from work to everything in the house tied up and knotted together with various nylon ropes and cords and long pieces of twine. "Someone untie the fridge so we can figure out dinner," I remember her yelling from the kitchen. (We ended up ordering pizza.)

"Get ready, Frankie!" Walter said, and hoisted me up out of a rocking chair I was sitting in. "Because we are going to ZIP-LIIIIIIIIIIIIIIIIIIIIIIIIINE!" His face did not look uncrazy.

"Oh god," I said. "You first."

Walter had engineered a kind of bucket seat—like a baby swing at the playground—by cutting leg holes in a plasticky blue Ikea tote bag. His plan was that we would take turns sitting inside the bag, with our legs sticking out of the holes, and the bag would hang from its handles on the rope and slide across it to the other side. When he'd first tried it, the handles ended up producing too much friction to slide easily, so Walter had slid them onto a metal towel bar and threaded the rope through the towel bar instead. The metal glided easily, and the idea was that the person's weight in the bag would keep the bag on the towel bar. Like I said, that was the idea, at least.

We were at the rope's high side, hoping to zip over the big open space in the middle of the warehouse. There was some display furniture set up in it, but Walter had calculated that we'd stay safely above it. He scampered up the metal shelving, climbing over all the stacked bins and boxes of furniture pieces, until he got to the top. Awkwardly—like he'd suddenly turned into a baby giraffe—he loaded himself into the seat, first one leg and then the other, even though the swing started sliding before his second leg was all the way in. He zipped across the warehouse, first yelling "I'm not readyyyyyy!" and then "This is awwwwwwesome!" until he slammed into the shelving on the other side. "Wowza!" he said. "Rough landing, but that was AWE-SOME!"

"So you mentioned," I said. I was laughing, but I knew what was coming next. He'd already run back across the warehouse to me. "Come," he said, and took my hand. And what could I do but follow?

With much encouragement from Walter as he coached from behind me—"Don't look down. Up, up. Keep looking up and reaching up!"—I climbed the shelving. Walter had lugged back the towel bar and the bag-seat, and then helped me into the bag. I put both legs in the holes before I let go of the beam and grabbed on to the towel bar.

Nothing happened. I dangled from the bag, but the bag did not move down the rope. "It's stuck," Walter said. "Push off the shelf with your foot—really push." I did, and the metal bar started to slide, and I was—there is no other way to put this—flying! I was soaring! I was . . . falling. Walter made fun of me afterward, about how I just said "Oh!" kind of quietly, right before there was a terrible tearing sound as the bag ripped in half and I fell out—or started to fall, before grabbing onto the fabric rope itself and hanging there, one leg in the torn bag, my upper body clamped around the fabric for dear life while the towel rod clattered to the ground.

"Walter!" I yelled. And he said, "I see, I see, Frankie. Okay. All good. You're good. Hang on nice and tight." And he scurried down the metal shelving and disappeared. I looked down and wished I hadn't. "Walter?" I called, more frantic this time. No response. Or, I should say, no *voice* responded. Because there *was* an answer, if you count the unmistakable *beep-beep-beep* of a truck backing up.

19

Quiet Time (Walter-Style)

A minute later, there was Walter, my hero, driving up in a forklift. "Oh yes I did," he said, before I could say anything like, for instance, "Have you completely lost your *mind*?"

It was one thing to do wild stuff; it seemed like something completely else to, you know, get ourselves killed. He was smiling like a crazy person—like the crazy person he was turning out to be—and he stopped with a jolt as he got close to me. "Luckily, the keys were in it. And double luckily, it's the same as driving my grandfather's riding mower. Hang on tight, Franks." In a couple of jerky back-and-forths, he maneuvered the machine beneath me. "One sec. I gotcha. Hang on. I'm just going to push this . . ." The forklift zipped backward, veering off to the left. "Nope," Walter said. "Not that, apparently. Whoa, holy rear-wheel steering!" He inched back below me, said "This?" and pushed a lever, and the forks dropped to the concrete floor with a loud clatter. "This!" he said, moving the lever the other way, and the forks came up, making a nice, comforting hydraulic sound. I planted my feet on them as soon as they were within reach, and Walter gently lowered me to the floor. "That," he said, when I was safely back on the ground, "was epic."

I remembered my camera and thought to take a picture of Walter then, perched up in the seat of the forklift, with the warehouse lights shining behind him, his smile as wide as the world.

Did you ever do that art project when you were little—the one where you paint a colorful picture and then cover the whole thing with a black crayon? It always felt so worrying to me at first, like I was ruining it. But then there was that feeling of scratching off the crayon with a toothpick, and the color was still there where I scraped, still bright, maybe brighter, even, against the dark of the crayon. That was Walter in this moment. Not unchanged by his sadness, definitely not, but with all his Walterness still there, still bright against it.

We ate a handful of strangely salty LÖRDAGS-GODIS licorice fish while we discussed our next activity. "Maybe something, I don't know, *quieter?*" I said.

"There are those metal beams above the cafeteria," Walter said, grinning. "Beams, like *balance* beams! We could climb up and, you know, shimmy along near the ceiling!"

"Um, quieter," I said. "More like watering all those tragic plants we saw back in the greenhouse, but, you know, a little less boring than that."

"We could arrange a row of shopping carts and challenge each other to leap cart to cart around the store without ever touching the ground! Or, wait, we could ride the carts down the stairs, and—"

"Walter! Walter. In case you missed it, I just *fell off a zip line.*"

"Well, technically I rescued you before you actually fell, but right. Okay. I know just the thing. It's a surprise," Walter said over his shoulder while he dragged me back through couches and tables, bedding and chairs, and stopped short just inside a showroom bathroom. The walls were dark orange tile, and where a normal house would have just a regular sink for everyone to share and fight over, there were three separate sinks, like white mixing bowls, each one on its own little sink base, with a hook and a clean white towel hanging from it.

"Nice," I said. "Especially if each person in your family requires their own sink. But, um, this really *is* a quiet activity. You know, admiring the bathroom."

Walter looked at me and shook his head. "Frankie, you're changing," he said. "A week ago, you would have wanted to spend all night in here, touching every tile with your amazed finger." He laughed. "And now you're like, Ikea shmikea." I laughed too, although it was kind of true. Not Ikea shmikea, but that the niceness of the stuff had worn off a little. "Anyway," he continued, "this is not the whole of the plan. All will be revealed. Wait here."

And Walter trotted off. During the couple of minutes he was gone, I looked at something labeled TOILET BRUSH, which grossed me out—like someone had borrowed your toothbrush, but to clean the toilet.

Also, I worried. Not about the toilet brush! About how this crazy adventure would end. How were Walter and I going to get home? How were we going to get out of this without getting in trouble? (Note to self: if you hate, hate, hate getting in trouble, then don't secretly spend the night at Ikea.) We hadn't come up with a real plan for the back end. Our short list of ideas—and it was very short—included hitchhiking and taking the bus, but we were scared to hitchhike, and we didn't know if there was a bus. I'd made a mental note of the route as my parents were driving—but what were we going to do, walk the forty-five miles home along the highway? I think it seemed kind of inevitable, at least to me, that we'd end up calling our parents. That we'd get in huge trouble and just deal with it then. But I had not ever spoken this aloud to Walter. Honestly, I dreaded reminding him that our night would have to end.

My thoughts were interrupted by the hushed staticky sound of voices over a walkie-talkie. I grabbed mine and hit the power button. Nothing. I pressed *talk*. "Walter," I whispered. "Come in, Walter." Nothing. I fiddled with the volume knob, wiped the antenna on my shirt, held the speaker up to my ear. Still nothing.

"Walter," I said, one more time, louder, "Come in, Walter." "Frankie," his voice boomed—in my other ear, where he had crept up to scare me. "Geez, Walter," I said, and he laughed. "I swear I heard something." Walter shrugged and shook his head. "Just me and my awesomeness!" He spread out the stuff he'd returned with: four large watering cans, a packaged tub plug, and two fluffy white NJUTA bathrobes.

"Don't tell me," I said. "Let me guess. Oh my gosh! Gardening in bathrobes? Did you think I was serious about watering the plants?"

"Duh. No," Walter said. "Can you say *pool party*?" I looked at him. I looked at the bathtub he was pointing to. The regular-size bathtub.

"We can take turns," Walter said. He was already fitting the plug into the drain. "There's no plumbing in the demo bathrooms, as we already found out the hard way," he said, and I laughed, remembering Zeke. "So we'll just pop out to the real bathroom to fill up these cans with water, fill the tub that way. The pool, I mean. Good?" I couldn't really think why not, although I did not have the best feeling about this plan.

There were many things that should have alerted

us to potential problems. For example: you never really think about how much water is in a bathtub until you are filling it with watering cans. And the paradox is that a watering can full of water is crazily heavy, yet it seems to add only a microscopic amount of water when you pour it into a tub. We made many trips, and decided to be satisfied with about ten inches of water, which was not the original goal. Also, not to be super picky, but in catalogs the bathtubs are always filled with water that glows a magically enticing pale blue-green. But somehow the water we'd poured in had a kind of dirty scum floating on it, maybe from the dust inside the showroom. It didn't give off a real "Leap in!" vibe.

I was also starting to think that sitting in ten inches of lukewarm water in Ikea, where you are not supposed to be, in the middle of the night might not—spoiler alert!—be really that fun. "This is such an awesome idea . . . ," I started to say.

"I'm sensing a big *but* coming on," he said. He'd put a robe on over his clothes for no reason I could tell, and belted it. "You are not feeling this plan, Frankie. Maybe what we need is a pitcher and some glasses, maybe some twinkle lights, to get more of a party vibe going—" He stopped short and looked at me. I was sitting on the closed lid of the toilet with my camera, taking a picture of him in his robe. "Wait," he said. "Did you hear that?"

And yes. Yes, I did.

20

What the Heart Says

Now Walter and I were hiding behind a shower curtain in the demo bathroom next door to our swimming-pool bathroom, shaking and chattering like Shaggy and Scooby. If I'd had a tail, you would have seen it sticking out from the curtain, shivering in fear. "I am wearing a bathrobe," Walter whispered to me. "I am in a real bathrobe in a fake bathroom in the middle of the night." I laughed, put a hand over my mouth. Then I saw Walter's eyebrows pull together. "What?" I said, and he shook his head. He pointed, and then I saw it too.

It was a dark line on the floor, and it was moving toward us. It was . . . what?

It was *water.*

Here's a tip: if you have the dubious sense to half fill a furniture-store demonstration tub, and then you spook yourselves thinking that you hear someone again on the walkie-talkies, do not—as you are scooping up your backpacks and dashing away, one of you wearing a bathrobe—stop to absentmindedly unplug the tub's drain. Just. Don't.

Ironically, given how shallow we'd filled the tub, it turned out to be a lot of water when it all came flooding out—through the drain that was connected to exactly nothing. "Um, did you unplug the tub, Franks?" Walter whispered, and he smiled at me sadly after I nodded. "Drains don't work so great without the pipes and stuff," he whispered, and this was definitely true.

We grabbed armfuls of bath towels from all the nearby displays and mopped up the floor as best we could, but yikes. It was a lot of water. When we were about half-done, Walter suddenly stopped and put a finger to his lips. "Shhh."

"What?" I whispered. He shook his head and said, "I thought I heard someone sighing! I'm probably just imagining it—imagining how my mom would respond to this. You know. *Sighingly.*"

But honestly? I'd heard it too—or I thought I had.

When we were finished with the mopping up (or at least we had done our best), we had a ginormous pile of wet towels. "Does Ikea sell appliances?" Walter asked, and I shook my head. "They sell kitchen stuff, but not, like, washers and dryers. If you're picturing tossing this stuff in a dryer." Instead, we found a package of TORKIS clothespins and hung the wet towels from our rigged-up fabric zip line. Once they were all clipped on, we stood back to admire the wet towels hanging like flags. It looked like a really awful party decoration, put up by giants. Giants who weren't feeling especially festive.

"Do you think we can just go relax somewhere?" I said, and Walter nodded.

"Maybe where the kids' stuff is?" he said. "Without the actual kids in it, it seems like it would be very relaxing." I laughed.

That area had been especially overstimulating for Zeke. When we'd walked through it earlier in the day, he'd fallen in love with one of the stylish pretend kitchens. He'd stood at the little stove for ages, rattling mini pots and pans, and every time we'd tried to lure him away, he'd said, in his little-kid yelling voice, "Guys! Guys! I can't go yet. I'm cooking! Guys! I'm COOKING!" "Okay, Zekey," we'd said. "As soon as you're done." But what with the felt cauliflower that needed frying and the pretend kiwi and cupcakes that needed getting turned into a salad, he was never done, and we finally had to pick him up and carry him out. He was still talking about it in the checkout line. I was holding him and he stuck his bottom lip out. "Guys!" he yelled, his mouth, like, an inch away from me. "Guys! I was COOKING! Remember? When I was cooking? GUYS! REMEMBER?"

We did! We remembered.

"Zeke, honey," Alice had said, laughing. "Frankie is right there! You really don't need to yell into her face like that."

"I'M SORRY, FRANKIE!" Zeke yelled into my face, and then he'd flung his little arms around my neck and squeezed. It's so straightforward for little kids. What they're feeling is not, like, a big puzzle you have to solve. It's all just right out there. It seems like kind of a shame that we're supposed to grow out of that style of expressing ourselves. I mean, it would definitely save a lot of time if you could just shout your feelings into somebody's face. "I hear you," they could say. And they would mean it literally.

Now the kids' section was illuminated in the prettiest way with all the lighting that was on display there, everything aglow: strings of heart-shaped lights and strings of miniature white globes; nightlights shaped like moons and stars, lightning bugs and flowers. There was a hanging blue lamp with white clouds on it and a clear lit-up box and colorful rubbery animals—like bears or mice or maybe Japanese comic-book creatures—shining softly all in a row. When I think about it now, I wonder why we weren't suspicious. I mean, why would all the kids' lighting have been left on like that, so enticingly? Plasticky, colorful lights: we were drawn to them like fish to a worm—fish to a worm *on a hook*. We had no idea.

"Why would you make a nightlight shaped like a *banana*?" Walter asked.

"Crescent moon," I said, and he said, "Ah."

It was so much fun to look at everything—all the stuff we'd kind of outgrown but still half wanted: the tea sets and stuffed mice and felt cupcake sets; the sidewalk chalk and rolls of white art paper; the tool sets and doll beds and wooden trucks.

Walter held up a set of watercolors. "'Watercolor cakes,'" he read. "That's so not what kids think it's going to be. You really picture, you know, *cakes*. Maybe in kind of swirly colors, but definitely with frosting and everything. Not just dried-up little disks of paint."

"It's mean," I agreed.

"Ooooh," he said. "Want to play the picking game? With the actual things?" I couldn't resist. My head was quieting down. Being here with Walter, everything calm now and softly lit, was like our night's intermission. I loved it.

Walter picked the DUKTIG 8-Piece Salmon Set, which was a little pretend serving dish with a fabric fish and stuffed lemon wedges and felt parsley sprigs. "It's just so awesomely twisted!" Walter said, studying it. "On one side, look, it's a live fish, with scales and fins and an eye and stuff, but then flip it over and it looks like lox. How super creepy for a little kid to play with—*Now it's a living creature, now it's food!*—but maybe I'm just thinking like a vegetarian."

I picked the miniature dollhouse-size set of Ikea furniture. It was so cool and perfect that I kind of couldn't stand it. There was a little pink couch, and a KALLAX bookcase, and a molded plastic chair, and even a tiny version of the classic Ikea red heart pillow with the arms outstretched. You could play Ikea right in Ikea, and thinking of it gave me a brain-twisting fun-house feeling. In a good way.

We walked around, looking at the play tents and bunk beds and art supplies. A lot of the kids' stuff was not as nice, in our opinion, as the adults' stuff: too many primary colors, too much plastic and busyness. We were more about sleek and stylish. But I still wanted to sit inside a play tent (which we did), and Walter wanted to make a huge rainbow with the MÅLA glitter paints (which we did). There was an open package of those melty beads that turn into a kind of plastic version of a drawing when you heat them. I arranged a portrait of Walter that made him look like a squared-off robot, and I tried to melt it in the cafeteria microwave, but it smoked in a bad way, and I was worried about setting off the smoke alarm or, worse, the sprinkler system. Anyway, in my haste to grab the melty-bead thing out of the microwave, I burned my fingers, and Walter pro-duced a Band-Aid from his first-aid kit with a trium-phant "Ta-da!"

We were getting tired, even though neither of us said this out loud. You could just tell. There was a real window, and I could see the real moon shining outside, a slivery little crescent. It gave me such a lonely feeling.

Walter and I climbed into the castle-themed bunk bed to rest awhile. It had a heavy velvety curtain around it, and we clicked on our headlamps so we could see better. It was quiet, and I could smell Walter's Walter smell—soap or shampoo, skin, and washed T-shirt—as comfortingly familiar to me as anything I know.

There was a little shelf running alongside the mattress, showing you all the nice things you could keep near your bed: the picture books and a stuffed hedgehog, the ladybug nightlight and a super-classic alarm clock with the double bell on top. There was also a framed photo of a smiling family.

I picked up the frame to look more closely, and Walter said, "That's kind of weird."

"What's kind of weird?"

"I don't know." Walter took the frame out of my hands and squinted at the picture. "It just kind of weirdly looks like your family. More than just the fact of it being a mom, a dad, and a girl about our age."

He was right. It was kind of uncanny. The dad had black-and-silver hair, like my dad, and the same squarish chin and big glasses. The mom was super smiley, like my mom, with her same curly reddish hair and even, I think, the exact same turquoise-and-red-striped cardigan my mom wears all the time. And the kid? I can't even explain it, but she was just so *me*. Not just the curly blond hair and the freckles. Not just the gray hoodie and jeans. And not just the exact same brown-and-green eyes as mine, but that was part of it. The eyes. Because this girl was looking out at me, I swear. She sat on a green velvet couch in between her parents, and they each had an arm slung around her shoulder, everyone smiling and happy, and she looked me in the eyes, and I felt all the excitement hiss out of me, like I was an inflatable raft that had gotten unstoppered.

It's true that I was also extremely tired. It was, I'm guessing based on what happened next, past three in the morning by this point—maybe even later. Walter was still looking at the photo, talking about how in the book we'd write this would be the creepy moment when the girl realizes that there's a magic photo of her family right there in the store. "It'd be like the *Titanic* movie, with the murder plot. Remember? How we were like, 'Seriously? They had to add a murder plot? Because the sinking of the world's most ginormous ship wasn't enough of a story?' People will be like, 'It wasn't enough that the kids spent the night in Ikea—there had to be a haunted snapshot?'"

But honestly? I was barely listening. I was still holding the picture, thinking about my parents. My parents, who I loved and trusted—and who loved me and trusted me back. I pictured them warm in their bed, asleep and dreaming, certain that I was safe and sound at Walter's house. And I was suddenly more homesick than I'd ever been in my life. Like, if you took all the homesickness in the entire world and boiled it down into a teaspoon and gave it to me to swallow—that's how homesick I was. Homesick and tired and worried and sad. I didn't want to hurt them, not at all. I just had so badly wanted to do something *apart* from them—to do this thing that we were doing, that we'd already done, on our own. To be free, in a way. Just Walter and me with our secret plan.

There's this place near my house where you can rent mini garages to keep your stuff in. The sign says SELF-STORAGE, and it confused me so much when I was little. We were driving past it one day when I was probably six or seven, and I asked my dad, "Why do people want to store their selves?" and my dad said, "What?" "*Self-storage*," I said. "Do you just, like, sit inside a bin or a box or what?" My dad had laughed and laughed and interrupted himself only long enough to say, "I'm

150

not laughing *at* you!" before laughing some more and then, finally, wiping his eyes and explaining that it was just a place where you could store your own stuff. I was offended, the way little kids can be when they're confused about something. "Maybe they should call it *stuff storage,* then," I said, mad, and my dad said, serious again, "Maybe they should." But every now and then that phrase floated back into my head. *Self-storage.* Sometimes it felt like that's what people were doing. What I was doing, even.

There's a sign all over Ikea, one that encourages you to think and rethink your purchases—to get more or different stuff than what you planned—and it's a picture of a red heart with open arms. There was one on the wall above the bed where we were. The heart sign. And what it actually said was, IT'S OKAY TO CHANGE YOUR MIND.

21

The Best-Laid Plans That Aren't Even Laid That Well

I climbed out of the bunk bed and stood on the floor with my elbows on the bed frame, my head just inside the curtain. I was thinking about how to tell Walter that I really didn't want to be there anymore—that I wanted to call it a night, go home, see my parents—but then I looked at him and he was smiling. Actually, he was squinting too, putting his arm up to block the glare of my headlamp, which was shining right into his eyes. I clicked it off.

I could still see his goofy smile, even in the dark.

And I couldn't say anything. I was too happy to be reunited with this version of my old friend. I didn't want it to end.

"What?" he said. "You had your Frankie-about-to-say-something eyebrows. What were you going to say?"

"Nothing," I said.

He smiled at me. "Were you going to say, 'Let's plug in a DANSA disco ball and light some candles and have a serious dance par-tay?' " Walter grabbed my hands and wiggled around crazily. Dancing was not so much his area of expertise—or mine.

I laughed. "I was going to say that exact thing, Walter. How did you know?"

The disco ball was easy. It has its own little lights that shine when you plug it in, and it spun around so prettily, silver and shiny and scattering its little squares of brightness all over the room. We really didn't even need the candles. Oh, but we couldn't stop ourselves! Ikea sells a lot of candles. Like, a million kinds of candles (not literally). We set up giant beeswax pillars and a ton of little votive candles in colored glass holders and some gorgeous long tapers in a big kind of glamorous candelabra, which looks like a menorah but from an elegant haunted house. (We knew all the proper candle terminology from—you guessed it—studying the catalog.) We hung up the pretty patio lantern I'd seen earlier, put some flower-shaped floating candles in a glass bowl of water and filled canning jars with candles. And then we lit them all.

At some point, my dad had hacked my Swiss Army knife for me. He removed the toothpick ("If you are ever really dying to pick your teeth, you can always whittle down a twig," he explained) and replaced it with a skinny magnesium fire steel. When you strike the steel sharply with the back of the knife, you make a nice, big spark that will catch a pile of wood shavings. Or that's the idea—but it's finicky and hard to use. You need to make a little pile of tinder and blow on it, and I was just starting to tear up a tissue into a pile of fluff when Walter said, "Seriously, Frank?" and pulled a pack of matches from his backpack.

"Or that," I said, and Walter laughed.

We lit two candles, then used them to light all the others. Then we unplugged the rest of the lights except for the disco ball.

"Wow," we both whispered, stepping back to look, and then, "Jinx."

It felt less like a dance party and more like a really

cool silent film or a bad music video with the sound off. Walter, swaying around in the quiet candlelight, looked like a weird dancing mime.

"I think I'd feel more like dancing if there were, you know, *music,*" I said.

So we looked for some. We found a tambourine, which Walter banged on exuberantly for a minute before shaking his head and grimacing, putting it back on the shelf. We found something called a MUSIK wall lamp, but there didn't appear to be anything musical about it. We found stereo wall units with no stereos in them. In fact, the only thing that seemed at all promising was a LEKA musical sheep—the kind of baby toy where you pull its tail and it plays a tinkly little lullaby. Walter and I sat on the floor, taking turns pulling its tail. I think—or I should say I *thought*—we were feeling the same thing: sleepy and little and done with adventure. Everything winding down. I could have closed my eyes. I *did* close my eyes.

"Woozy?" Walter asked, and I smiled.

Before he died, Walter's dad had been losing language like a snake shedding its skin. Meanings fell away from words, and sometimes he would latch onto a single word for an hour or half a day, use it for everything,

155

like it was a kind of all-purpose part of speech. As long as you rolled with it—without pressuring him to find the right word—he didn't get too frustrated. One day a new word started when he was resting on the couch with his usual mug of tea, the late-afternoon sun slanting in through the window. Walter and I were sitting at the coffee table, designing a board game that involved dice and salted peanuts, and that we were calling the Hunger Game.

"Sweetie," Walter's dad said to Walter, "would you mind . . . could you please . . ." He gestured with his hand. ". . . woozy that . . . woozy?" Walter touched the bottle of fizzy water on the table. "Woozy *this* woozy, Dad?" "No, no," his dad said patiently, and shook his head, tried pointing again, squinted. "That woozy." "This woozy?" Walter said, standing up to touch the window shade, and his dad nodded and laughed. "That woozy," he said, and shook his head while Walter lowered the shade. "Perfect. But it's not the woozy, I know," he said. "Woozy," he said again, and raised his eyebrows, and we laughed.

A little later, he leaned forward to shake the can of peanuts, then sighed and said, "It would have been nice to have some more woozies, right?" "Nuts?" I said. And he shook his head and said, "Cousins." Walter and I had started to use the word *woozy* when we couldn't think of exactly what we wanted to say.

I opened my eyes. "It's better now, right?" I asked hopefully. I can remember when it felt like grief was radiating out from Walter. Like if he'd been a cartoon, you would have seen wavy lines coming off him. It didn't feel like that now. Or not as much, at least.

Walter was quiet for a bit, then he nodded. Then he shook his head.

"I don't know," he said. "The only thing it's kind of like is this poem I read. It's about a person you love dying? And the poem compares it to a house burning down—how at first you're like, 'Oh no! I really loved that house!' And then you start to realize that the house was also full of all this other stuff you loved, only now it's all gone. All your favorite pictures and dishes and books. All burnt up in the burnt-down house. Does that make sense?"

"Kind of," I said carefully, even though it didn't really.

"Like, at first, it's the idea that this person you love

is gone—that's what's so terrible. *He's never coming back. My father is dead.* And it's the worst, or you think it is. Because then the actual missing him is the actual worst—not the simple fact of his goneness. Like, I miss him when he doesn't make pancakes on the weekend. I miss him when he doesn't tell stories to me and Zeke at bedtime. I miss him when I can't put my arms around his neck and dangle down his back. I miss his shaving smell, and his voice, and his laugh. And all those things are gone, and where they were there are just these giant holes instead, and all you can do is kind of . . . fall into them and break your leg every five minutes."

Walter turned toward me then—he'd been staring into his lap while he was talking—and I must have looked terrified or heartbroken, because he was quick to reassure me. "It's okay, Frankie," he said. "It's not as bad as I'm making it sound."

"I don't know if I should pretend to believe you," I said. And Walter said, "You totally should."

I stretched out onto my back to look up at the little squares of light that were still moving around the walls of our silent disco. I wanted to say something deep to Walter, something that would make him feel understood by me, but instead I said, "Remember when my mom did all that recipe testing that was just about *toast?*"

"Totally," Walter said. "I was just thinking about that."

And we lay there quietly reminiscing about rye and challah, oatmeal and honey-wheat, until Walter sighed and said, "I practically *smell* toast!" Which was when we realized that the curtains were on fire.

22

Hello?

We started a fire, and our night went up in smoke.

"Oh my god," I said. "Oh my god oh my god oh my god." I was trying to stamp out the fire with my foot, although it had already climbed up the curtain, which was blazing and crackling now. I was afraid of setting my hair on fire. "Walter?" I said, or maybe yelled. Where was he? Maybe he was blowing out all the candles. "Walter?" I yelled his name again, just as a horrible siren started blaring. The fire alarm! It was like a flock of a million geese all honking at once, in a really high-pitched way, over and over again. A bright white light was flashing from the wall, and the siren was screaming, and I was panicking, trying to pull the curtain down from the demo curtain rod.

We were going to be in *such big trouble*. If we didn't get incinerated first.

And all of a sudden, there was Walter, leaping into view with—yes—a red fire extinguisher in his hands. "Kiai!" he yelled, like he was in our old karate class, about to kick his foot out. He *did* kick his foot out. Then he spun around, spraying whiteness everywhere. It was a huge cloud of white powder, and I couldn't see a thing—just the horrible flashing light, just the lick of flames at the edge of the powder fog. Just the . . . I looked up and—"Oh no!"—saw one of the sprinkler heads near the ceiling lower itself and spin partway around, felt a drop of water, felt dizzy, pictured water showering down from all the ceilings, across the entire store, drenching everything like the world's worst in-door Swedish thunderstorm.

But the cloud of fire-extinguisher stuff was settling and clearing, and Walter was triumphantly leaping into the air. "It's out!" he yelled over the noise of the alarm. "It's out!" And it was. The flames were gone, the cur-tain hanging black and white and steaming. The alarm stopped. The light went off. The head of the sprinkler screwed itself upward, popped back up into the ceiling with a click. Walter blinked at me. It was dark now, but he was dusted in powder, practically glittering. And he was grinning again, even though, oh my god, we were in so much trouble now. There was really no way around that fact anymore. "Walter," I said, just as he grabbed my arm.

"Did you hear that?"

"Hear what?" I said. But just at the moment I did, in fact, hear it. Something. Footsteps? Quiet ones, but definitely footsteps.

There was a pair of hanging EKORRE chairs— they're like a cross between a tent and a swing—and Walter shoved me toward one, then jumped into the other. We scrunched down into the swaying cocoons as far as we could, and I more or less held my breath.

I could hear the footsteps getting closer, like in a scary movie. They were about the same loudness as the sound of my heart banging away in my ears. Maybe it was just my heart banging? My brain was too scrambled to figure anything out.

"Hello?" This was not my heart banging. This was a real-live human voice. "Hello?"

23

That Scene I Mentioned at the Very Beginning

I couldn't see Walter's feet hanging out of his chair anymore. "If that's you, Walter, I am going to kill you," I whispered, but Walter didn't whisper back.

Because it wasn't Walter. The footsteps stepped into my line of vision, and I saw a person reach a hand out to touch the still-smoldering curtains. I saw a navy-blue shirt tucked into belted navy-blue pants, a matching navy-blue cap, a flashlight the size of a tree limb in one hand.

Security guard.

There was a folded piece of paper in the other hand, and I cringed to recognize it. Our stupid note about the pillows. If I hadn't been trying to be quiet, I would have slapped my own forehead. Not that it really mattered at this point, I guess. It's not like the fire wouldn't have given us away.

The person turned around. *She* did. It was a she. She drew a long arc with the beam of light, swinging it past us, then past us again the other way, then training it back and forth between the two chairs.

Zeke used to think that the way you played hide-and-seek was to sit in plain view of the seeker, but as still as possible, with your eyes closed—or maybe a dish towel draped over your head. If you did that, then they couldn't find you. He'd put a hand over his mouth to stifle his own loud giggling, as if that would really help when he was sitting there right in front of you, but honestly? That's what Walter and I were like now. The flashlight beam was on us, and we sat completely still, completely silent, like if we wished hard enough we would become invisible.

And in case you were wondering? We did not become invisible.

"Mixed-up files," I heard Walter whisper. Indeed,

yes. If we could have terminated our mission then and disappeared into thin air, I'm sure we would have.

The person spoke. "So, you thought you'd light a fire," she said, and shook her head. "You thought you'd break into Ikea in the night and make a huge mess and flood half the store and drive the forklift and then you thought, *Hey, let's set the whole freaking place on fire!*"

I sat, frozen in the beam of light. Paralyzed with fear. The guard's lips were so tightly pinched together now that they looked like narrow white lines. My stomach felt like it had a sack of marbles rolling around in it. "We didn't," I said, even though it wasn't what I meant to say and, also, was stupid. And then I said, panicky, "We did." I couldn't turn my chair around to see Walter, but I imagined he looked as panicky as I felt.

The security guard sighed and angled her light down a little so that it wasn't shining right in our eyes. "I'm not going to hurt you," she said, as if we were wild animals. "Why don't you guys come out of there, and we can start to figure this out."

We climbed out of the chairs. Or tried to. It turns out to be very, very hard to climb out of a swinging chair when you're freaking out. I got my leg caught and ended up tipping myself out backward, while Walter

165

somehow dove toward the floor headfirst, his butt sticking up in the air. While he tried to free his sneakers, his butt kept bobbing up and down, and it was not elegant. The security guard actually had to put her light down and help us, saying, "Wait, hold on a sec," while she untangled our legs and clothing. You could tell she was trying not to laugh, but she was chuckling a little anyway. "Yikes!" she said, and "Oof. Hang on."

By the time we were freed, the three of us were sitting on the floor, and she was smiling. "I'm Shirley," she said. "Security guard. Civilian personnel." She put out her hand, and we each shook it.

"Walter," Walter said quietly. And I said, "I'm Frankie," and then added, pointlessly, "We're in sixth grade."

"Nice to meet you," Shirley said, and then we sat quietly for what felt, uncomfortably, like a hundred hours.

Shirley stood up finally, walked over to the wall, and flipped on some of the overhead lights. Walter and I blinked in the brightness.

"Sooo," Shirley said, and shrugged. She sat down with us again. "Maybe you first? I mean, I've been working here a long time, since this place opened, and

I can tell you—I have never met any kids in the night before. Never met anybody in the night, actually. Well, there was a stray cat who snuck in to have her kittens in a basket. But other than her. So, yeah, anyway." She smiled, raised her eyebrows, waited.

This was not the movie scene I would have imagined, with mean, angry cops, everybody yelling, Walter and me terrified as they pushed us into a car, yanking us around by our hair and clothes. In fact, what I felt more than anything was relief. This was bad, in a way, and it was going to get worse, I imagined. And yet, I had been so filled with dread about trying to get Walter to leave—it was almost reassuring that I had a way out now, one that wasn't my idea.

"Did you turn all the pretty lights on for us?" Walter asked. And Shirley nodded.

"I did." Shirley was sitting in that awkward cross-legged way that grown-ups sit, where you can tell they're not used to sitting on the floor. I could see her black socks.

"Like a trap or to be nice?" Walter asked.

"Uh, to be nice, I guess," she said, and cringed. "But I probably should have stopped you guys a long time ago."

"You sighed once," Walter said. "I heard you." Shirley shrugged, smiling.

"Wait. Did you *call* us?" Walter said. And Shirley said, "What?"

"On the phone," Walter said, then shook his head. "Nothing. Forget it." It was silent again.

"This is not what you think," I finally said, because I couldn't bear the silence and because that's what people always say: *It's not what you think!* But also because I thought it was true.

"Uh . . ." Shirley shook her head a little. She half smiled. "You're not in Ikea in the middle of the night?"

"No, no. I mean, yes, we're here, obviously." I laughed a little. I felt like words were just going to spill out of me into a puddle of nervous talking. "But we're not, like, runaways or anything. We just had this idea about spending the night here. We read this book once—oh, well, it's kind of a long story. But I just mean we're actually happy kids. Happy kids from happy homes. Not, like, escaping some horrible orphanage or, like, terrible parents or anything. I just mean . . ." What did I mean? "I just mean, it's bad, what we did, but it doesn't mean anything bad about our lives."

Shirley nodded and smiled, but Walter was shaking his head. "No," he said.

Maybe it was because of the light, or maybe it was because of the fire-extinguisher powder that still clung to him, but his face looked more gray than the warm, familiar brown I was used to. I felt my chest tighten—felt the word *cage* inside *rib cage*.

"Walter," I said, and scooched closer to him.

"No, no, no," he said. "Don't." His voice broke on *don't*. I didn't understand.

"Don't *what?*" I said. "Walter," I said again.

He was sitting with his long giraffe legs crossed, and he bent over them and covered his face with his hands. I pressed my palm onto his back, and Shirley looked politely away while Walter started to cry.

24

Walter, Again

Walter cried. He cried and cried, not loud, but hard—the kind of crying that makes your shoulders quietly shake and shake. I sat with my arm around him, feeling helpless.

I thought about what my own dad had said pretty soon after Walter's dad died. I'd come home from their house one day, sat down on the couch, and burst into tears. "I can't do anything to help," I'd said. "Walter is just sad, and I go over, and he's sad, and I leave, and he's just as sad as he was before. I don't know what to do."

"You're already doing it," my dad had said gently.

"You just keep showing up and showing up. It's all you can do, and it doesn't feel like it's helping, but it is. Just being there is the most important thing."

And so I kept showing up. And I had imagined it had gotten better.

But now I was starting to think I didn't know. *Self-storage*. Maybe Walter was storing his self too. I didn't know everything—only the parts that I'd seen. That he'd shown me.

Walter cried and I held him and Shirley looked away. "He's sad," I explained stupidly. Like, in case she couldn't tell. Eventually, she stood up and went somewhere, came back with a cup of water and a box of tissues, which she set down gently on the carpet. Her forehead was creased with worry, and I liked her for that.

Poor Walter. He laughed at some point, from underneath his crying, and said, "Snot everywhere," and I passed him a tissue. Then he sat up and wiped his face on his sleeve. "I'm not going back," he said, and hiccuped, and Shirley nodded gently. "I can't," he said. He cried a little more then, like an extra shower after a rainstorm, and then he said, "I can't go back. She's so sad. Frankie, you have no idea. She just cries all the time. She thinks we're asleep, but we're not, and she just cries and cries in her bed, where we usually are too. Then Zeke cries because she's crying, but she can't comfort him, so he presses up into me and cries, and he drapes himself all over me, crying, and everyone is crying except me, because someone has to comfort them, and it's awful."

He put his head in his hands again. "The only person who'd be able to help her is my dad. But, of course, he's not there. Because he's dead, which is why everyone's crying. And I miss him so much, but I don't even really talk about it ever because I don't want to make it worse." His words had come out in a rush, but now he stopped talking and hiccuped again.

"Walter," I said again. Walter. My Walter. He was right. I had no idea.

In *Mixed-Up Files*, Claudia says that people end up telling their secrets because it's no fun to have a secret and not tell it. But this was not that kind of secret. This was the dull, aching kind of secret that was just your own untold feelings, rusting away in your brain. In your heart.

"I'm not going back," Walter said again. He picked

at some invisible something in the carpet. "You can go, Frankie, but I'm not going with you."

"I don't even know what you mean," I said. "I mean, I know what you mean about how bad it is at your house. But I don't understand what you're saying about staying, what your plan is."

Walter shrugged. "I don't know," he said, and then, because he's always totally his own sweet-hearted self, "Shirley, will it be complicated for you, my not leaving here?"

Shirley nodded slowly, chuckled a little. "Um, yep," she said. "Pretty complicated." She took off her hat then, held it in her lap, and smoothed her short dark hair back from her forehead. "Look," she said. "It's none of my business, the part about your personal life? But I'll tell you something. I ran away too, when I was a little older than you guys. And I stayed run away. I didn't go home again after, and it's too long a story to explain. Let me just say I was not, uh, *supported* by my family." She ran her fingers through her hair, looked at us through her clear green eyes, and smiled. "I think that's why I left you alone for so long, maybe. It was not the right thing to do. I don't know what I was thinking. But I wanted you to have your time."

"Thank you," I said. And Shirley said, "You're welcome."

She continued. "Look, I'm definitely no therapist. I'm not even so great with feelings, which make me uncomfortable a little, I have to tell you. But, Walter, your dad died. That's a big deal. I'm sorry that happened. But I'm sure your family loves you. It's obvious your friends do, or at least this one does." She pointed at me. "Maybe you just need a little more time." Shirley sighed. Walter's shoulders felt still beneath my arm now. He was calmer. "I'm not just trying to talk you out of staying here," Shirley added. "Although, no, you can't stay here. I need to say clearly that you're minors, so it's all going to be okay, but it's fully illegal for you to be here. As in, against the law."

What had we done?

I had the strangest feeling of looking down at ourselves from far away, like an overhead camera zooming out: us on the carpet, in a showroom, in the concrete building, at the edge of the highway near our town, which was on this continent in the middle of the ocean, on the spinning blue-and-green planet. I think this might be called *vertigo*. If I hadn't been sitting down, I would have needed to sit down.

"I'll give you guys a minute to sort yourselves out," Shirley said. "But I'm going to have to call your parents. And we're going to need to figure out who's paying for all of this, and how." She gestured toward the burnt curtains, the burnt carpet. I thought of the ruined wall behind the couches, the exploded pillows.

Walter shook his head. "Ugh. I'm going to have to add *disappointed* to the list of my mom's unbearable feelings."

I pictured Walter's mom, with her face shining over the pieced-together Ikea birthday cake—her radiant love for him. "I don't think so," I said to him. "Maybe she just needs to, you know, wake up a little." I was thinking that that's exactly what Walter had needed to do too—had done. And maybe I had too.

"This will definitely wake her up," Walter said. "Especially the phone ringing." He sighed. "Okay," he said, and held out his wrists. "We're ready. Go ahead." When Shirley looked at him quizzically, he said, "Cuff us."

But she only laughed and said, "You wish."

25

Pins and Needles

What happened next was these things, in this order: (1) Shirley called my parents and Alice. (2) Walter persuaded Shirley to heat us up some meatballs, in a kind of prisoner's-last-meal scenario. (3) Walter ate vegetarian meatballs, and I ate meat ones. Shirley ate a few too, although she expressed her doubts about whether this was the right thing for her to be doing just then. "I almost never eat them anymore!" she said between bites. "But they really are good!" (4) The grown-ups and Zeke arrived in Alice's car an hour later, with messy hair and serious expressions.

Walter and I waited for everyone on the same

couch where we'd started the day. The day *before*, I guess I should say. Shirley wanted to meet them at the doorway, to talk to them alone first. I think she had a different picture of the kind of people they were—like they were going to come in furious and rage at us—but I was happy enough to have this last bit of time with Walter.

"It's like pins and needles, you know?" he said.

"What is?"

"When your feelings wake up." Walter laughed a little, shook his head. "You know, like when you're lying funny on your hand, and then you can't feel it. But then it comes back to life and it hurts. That's what it feels like. Prickly and painful." His voice got quiet. "But I think it's going to be better than the numbness."

We heard them just then, clattering up the stopped escalator. I saw my mom press her lips into a tight line when she saw us, shake her head. But she hugged me when I stood up, and Alice put her arms around Walter. My dad was holding Zeke, but he smiled at me. He either blinked funny just then or winked at me—I never found out which.

"I thought you were sleeping at Walter's," my mom said.

"I know," I said. "I wasn't."

"You *lied* to us," she said from inside my hair, which was where her face was.

"I did," I said. "I'm sorry."

"I am very happy to see you," she said, "but also I am totally killing you."

Walter and I sat on the couch with Zeke, who was asleep again and spread out over our laps, while the grown-ups talked in another room. We learned later that they were figuring out how we would pay for the damage we'd caused. Our parents were also asking Shirley what would happen next—if she'd need to explain the ruined things, tell someone what we'd done. Shirley didn't want to rat us out because we were such nice kids—but our parents were too mad to tell us that at the time. "I think it's just the couches that won't be sorted out by morning," Shirley told them, apparently. "And I can say that the top one didn't appear to be secured properly and fell down."

The light was just breaking at the edge of the horizon, a kind of gray glow, when Alice pulled the minivan out of the Ikea parking lot. Shirley was waving from behind the big automatic doors, and Walter and I waved back. "In *Mixed-Up Files*, they go home in a Rolls-Royce," I said, sighing, and Walter laughed quietly.

We were in the back with Zeke, who was barely awake and kept patting Walter's arm, saying what Alice had said when we were walking out: "Sweetie, sweetie, never do that again. Promise me." "I promise you, Zekey-Deke," Walter said. And Zeke said, "You're my good boy," before falling asleep in his car seat. I craned my head around to see the blue-and-yellow Ikea sign behind us, getting smaller and smaller and then disappearing completely.

Walter and I were each holding a stuffed heart, the kind with arms and hands. Shirley had given them to us when we were leaving. She shook hands with each of us, then threw her arms around us both and whispered, "All you need is love. I didn't make that up, I know, but it's true." Later, I'd look at that heart on my bed, and I almost wouldn't believe what we'd done.

Alice dropped us off, and my parents ruffled my hair, said, "Let's talk more about all of it after we get a little sleep, okay?" and went into the house. I stood outside for just a second longer. There was still a tiny sliver of moon in the sky, but the sun was rising now, a glowing orange globe more perfect than anything you could ever buy, turning all the clouds pink around it. I heard a sound, felt a vibration on my back. "Frankie, Frankie, come in, Frankie."

The walkie-talkie. I dug it out of my backpack and pressed the talk button. "Walter!" I could still see the van, just turning off our street.

"Shirley was right." The voice came in crackly now, but I could hear him. Maybe he was crying again, or maybe it was just the bad connection. "She was right, Frankie. You and me. We've got everything we need."

And in that moment, it was true. We did.

26

After

A lot of things changed after that night—besides our parents keeping a closer watch on us and asking *a lot* more questions about what we were doing and when we'd be back.

Most important, Walter and his mom started seeing a family therapist, and things were getting better at their house now: sometimes they were sad, yes, but there were no more secrets, no more late-night tears, no more smothered feelings. The lighter Walter seemed, the more I understood the weight that had been on him, like he'd been carrying a rolled-up carpet across his shoulders for half a year.

We didn't tell a lot of people about our night at Ikea. There were parts of it that felt too private and parts that felt too crazy to be believed. We'd been planning to write a story about it and try to sell it, to pay for the damages. But in the end we didn't. We just did more of the jobs we were already doing: I doubled up on my babysitting hours, and Walter added another cat to his summer cat-feeding rotation in the neighborhood. We'd get it paid for.

Well, not the damage we'd actually done, because Shirley took care of explaining it to corporate headquarters or whatever. But we'd agreed to earn the cost of fixing the broken wall and donate it to an organization for runaway teens that Shirley was very involved with. This seemed like a pretty perfect compromise to Walter and me. And we knew we'd gotten off easy.

My mom would bring it up from time to time, the Ikea night. "Sometimes I think of how we didn't even *know* that we didn't know where you were," she said once. "And it makes me so scared I can hardly breathe."

"I know," I said. "I'm really sorry about that."

She was quiet for a minute, nodding and chewing a forkful of salad. "Is it weird that there are raisins in the tuna salad? The raisin people want me to be some kind of Raisin Ambassador, which means I put raisins in everything and they pay me. I can't decide. Too raisin-y?" So: things were different now, but also the same.

We went to the beach a lot that summer, and my dad always packed up our stuff in one of the huge blue plastic Ikea bags with the yellow handles. I'd be lying on my towel, drying off in the sun, and I'd see the bag and remember our adventure almost like an electric shock. Of course, Walter was with us a lot, and he'd point at the bag and shake his head, like, *Crazy kids*, which we were.

Another good thing that happened is that Walter's family got a new kitten, a tiny little furball sister for Puddle. She was the cutest thing, sleeping in a salad bowl, attacking our feet, falling into the bathtub. Zeke wanted to name her Puddle, "like our own Puddle, who is the cat who I also love!" But Walter convinced Zeke to give her Puddle as a middle name—and he named her Shirley instead. "Shirley Puddle, the kitten of kittens," Alice called her.

Speaking of: we stayed in touch with Shirley, or our parents did, really, and she actually ended up coming to our Fourth of July barbecue. She brought a really nice person with her—someone with pretty blond hair, who loved to laugh and who Walter and I thought was probably her partner, though we weren't sure. I asked Walter if he thought Shirley had run away as a teenager because of having, or wanting, a girlfriend—it seemed so sad to me to imagine—and he shrugged and said, "You only know the things that people tell you." True enough. Maybe one day she would.

Later, I would find that I felt different about Ikea. I still loved it, and Walter and I still sat on our couches to play the picking game. We still got the wanties about everything, even. But we'd put our feet up on the coffee table, and I could also feel, alongside the fun, fizzy feeling of loving all the stuff, that I didn't actually want anything. Not really. I'd even gotten rid of some of my collections. I mean, just into a bin in the basement, but still.

I should mention, though, that the coffee table was new. Or, I should say, new as a coffee table. But let me back up. When you have done the world's craziest thing and been caught and had to explain everything? When your parents are as upset with you as mine were with me? That's a good time to tell them whatever else you've been holding back, because let's face it: in the context of us having spent the night in Ikea, the fact that I wanted a doorknob was really not that big a deal.

When I tried to explain, I could hear how big this felt to them, this small confession—as if it made sense of the whole Ikea adventure, fit all the puzzle pieces into a picture, for them, of the inside of my head. And you know, maybe it did. I saw them look at each other over my head—a Meaningful Look, as if they'd talked about it, or as if my saying I wanted a new door was the key that unlocked some big secret. It was very annoying. Very my parents. But I was glad that their feelings didn't seem to be too hurt. "You need a door," my mom said. "One that shuts. That's a perfectly reasonable thing to want. I'm sorry we didn't think of offering it to you."

My parents decided to remove the old door—they couldn't bear to screw anything into it—so I got to pick a new door and, yes, even the knob. I painted the wood a cool, modern color called Swedish blue, and my parents installed the door for me, cursing over the hinges and the hardware. We stood back to admire it, and then I said, "If you don't mind." And they said, "Please," and I stepped into my room, pushed the door, and heard the satisfying click of it closing. I loved it. A second later, there was a knock, my mom's voice saying, "Can I come in?" and then she said, through the closed door, "I'm totally kidding," and I heard her and my dad laughing.

My dad added smooth wooden legs to the beautiful old door and now it was a coffee table. Because it was a new spot to sit, it had immediately become Mr. Pockets's favorite place in the house, and he was sprawled there most evenings, among the cups and mugs, the games and books and catalogs. That coffee table was now the least Ikea thing in the whole house, but I loved it. I loved its dings and scrapes—"war wounds," my mom called them—and whatever secrets it held from all the families it had known. I even mostly loved our too-small house, my messy room, my imperfect parents and my imperfect life. It wasn't a lesson with a capital *L* or anything—but something had changed for me nonetheless.

I had new pictures in my room too. They were in Ikea frames (of course), and they were all from that night. That Night. One was a selfie we'd taken up in the loft, when we'd first gotten there, our cheeks smashed together, our eyes wide. One was of Walter in the white bathrobe, raising his eyebrows at me, which always made me laugh. Another was of Walter on the forklift. He's smiling in the picture, as bright as a shooting star, and the warehouse lights are shining behind him like a crazy halo. It was that whole night in one image. Or, you know, *practically* that whole night.

The last image was one Walter took—one that I didn't see until I'd downloaded my pictures onto the computer. It was of a heart drawn on a whiteboard easel in the kids' area, and inside it, in Walter's handwriting, were three words:

Thank you Frankie

And now, because I could say things out loud with my door closed, I whispered back, "It was my pleasure, Walter." And it was. Much more, even. Besides, what I really meant was "Thank *you*." So I said that too.

Thank You, Thank You, Thank You

My son, Ben, and his oldest friend, Ava, are Walter and Frankie to me, and I am so grateful to them for the dozen (plus) years they've spent lying around our house with the Ikea catalog, playing the picking game. Also for their beautiful example of friendship, which I mined for material. And to Ikea itself, because where else would Walter and Frankie really want to spend the night?

I wrote this book imagining my daughter, Birdy, as its audience, and she was its first and best reader. Her graceful intelligence and compassionate eye are so valuable to me.

My own oldest friend, the late, great Ali Pomeroy, died while I was writing this book, but not before giving Walter's dad all his best lines. Thank you, Al. I miss you all the time.

Also late and great: E. L. Konigsburg, author of *From the Mixed-Up Files of Mrs. Basil E. Frankweiler,* which was such an inspiration to Frankie and Walter (and me).

K.J. dell'Antonia was my one-woman writing group, and I wrote this book because I knew that every Friday she would email to see if I had written, and I was scared to say I hadn't. Thank goodness for K.J.! (And cowardice!)

The purring-est Craney Crow lent elements of his personality to both Puddle and Mr. Pockets, but he slept through most of his own helpfulness.

Many wonderful people read the book and/or offered up the bounty of their time, energy, or imaginations at crucial moments, including Jeanne Birdsall, Ava Blum-Carr, Jonathan Carr, Kelly Close, Sophia Corwin, Layla Elkalai, Cammie McGovern, Becky Michaels, Peter Michaels, Michael Millner, Jennifer Newman, Chris Perry, Jennifer Rosner, Brittany Shahmehri, and Kathleen Traphagen. Thank you.

Publishing a book means, of course, getting tons of help from people who are in the business of publishing books—but then they help you way more than their jobs technically require. My beloved agent, Jennifer Gates, is just that kind of above-and-beyond person, and she fought for this book in the most devoted way. Jennifer's colleague Rick Richter generously offered both encouragement and middle-grade expertise. Michelle Nagler, my brilliant editor at Random House, may actually love Frankie and Walter as much as I do, which I love her for, and she made sure that this book would shine for them. Her colleague Jenna Lettice also stepped in to offer vitally important feedback at a vitally important moment. Alison Kolani and her eagle eyes and eagle-eyed copy editors Barbara Bakowski and Diana Drew helped make the writing as good as it could be. And Ann Macarayan patiently designed the cover of my dreams.

My friends, my kids, my parents, and my husband are my best cheering squad. Thank you. Love is all you need. It really is.

About the Author

CATHERINE NEWMAN is the author of the memoirs *Catastrophic Happiness* and *Waiting for Birdy*, which are books written *for* adults *about* kids. This is her first book written *for* kids *about* kids. (YAY!) She lives in Amherst, Massachusetts—ninety miles from the nearest Ikea—with her husband, kids, cats, friends, and books. Visit her at catherinenewmanwriter.com.